'...and intriguing detail.'

METRO

'Murder mystery meets magical fantasy in this highly entertaining debut, rich in inventive world-building

A MESSAGE FROM CHICKEN HOUSE

Nicki Thornton is officially the Queen of Magical Crime! Here she's back with detecto-cat Nightshade to uncover a new mystery in a weird and wonderful village. There's a beginner witch, annoying new boys and some very strange goings-on. Will they be a match for the Howling Hag? Watch out for the twists and turns – and a few extra screams along the way!

BARRY CUNNINGHAM
Publisher
Chicken House

THE HOWLING HAG MYSTERY

NICKI THORNTON

2 PALMER STREET, FROME, SOMERSET BA11 1DS

Text © Nicki Thornton 2021
Illustrations © Héloïse Mab 2021

First published in Great Britain in 2021
Chicken House
2 Palmer Street
Frome, Somerset BA11 1DS
United Kingdom
www.chickenhousebooks.com

Chicken House/Scholastic Ireland, 89E Lagan Road, Dublin Industrial Estate,
Glasnevin, Dublin D11 HP5F, Republic of Ireland

Cover and interior design by Steve Wells
Cover and inside illustrations by Héloïse Mab
Typeset by Dorchester Typesetting Group Ltd
Printed and bound in Great Britain by CPI Group (UK) Ltd, Croydon CR0 4YY

FSC
www.fsc.org
MIX
Paper from
responsible sources
FSC® C020471

1 3 5 7 9 10 8 6 4 2

British Library Cataloguing in Publication data available.

PB ISBN 978-1-913322-70-0
eISBN 978-1-913696-14-6

For Pam and Ed

Also by Nicki Thornton

PART ONE

1. DENY EVERYTHING

Raven Charming knew there was only one Golden Rule in life.

If anything strange happened – unexpected good luck, objects moving by themselves, the blossoming of inexplicable smells – Mum said just to remember the Golden Rule: Deny Everything.

Which wasn't always easy to follow, particularly when you had a sister like Rookery. Luckily for Raven, most people believed that everything about witches belonged in fairy tales.

Mum was the wisest person Raven knew. She had a busy and important job finding obscure cures for unfortunate people. Raven never liked to bother Mum, not with the sort of unimportant questions she puzzled over. How had Henry VIII's sixth wife died? Where was the second of her lucky polka-dot socks? Was there a spell to get rid of freckles? Or how to stop new boys firing jets of cold water at you as you cycled past ...

This was the one bothering Raven right now as she prepared to cycle up to Grandpa Knox's after school: how to deal with the new threat in town? The annoying boy who would be waiting on the shadowy side of the Howling Hag Inn with his beaming grin and deadly accuracy with a water gun.

Raven pedalled furiously as she left Twinhills School. With its red-painted metal and glass structure and pointy roof, the school sat brashly in the middle of the sleepy high street. It sprawled with confidence, taking up more than its fair share of room among the snug cottages either side that looked as if they had huddled up closer to make space.

She flew past her head teacher's overly orderly house, which always gave her the shivers, and by the time she got to the Howling Hag she was really moving. The pretty inn at the centre of Twinhills was made of bricks the colour of butter, with a low roof and tiny windows. Pretty, except for the unfortunately ugly pub sign of a hideous wart-faced old woman with a black cat and a broomstick. At least it offered chips, even on a Sunday.

As she reached the Howling Hag she braced herself for the jet of icy water she knew was coming. Then, right at the last second, Raven changed her mind and put on the brakes hard.

Last night she'd broken one of her own golden rules and interrupted Mum at her big, cluttered desk, glasses perched on the end of her nose, poring over a load of old books and scrolls as she tried to work out how to turn chocolate cutlery back into silver. Finch Charming had removed her glasses and chewed on one of the ends, considering Raven's question.

'The new boy is squirting water at you? The one whose lovely mum and dad have taken over the village inn? They brought a whole pizza to the youth club on Friday.' Mum had put her glasses on top of her head, knocking her topknot at a precarious angle. 'He's new in Twinhills. He's probably doing it to get your attention. Maybe just try to be friendly?'

'Friendly? With the person who is squirting water at me?' Raven had repeated, just to be clear that she had not misunderstood, and hoping Mum might tell her she needed a biscuit to cheer herself up. Finch Charming was the sort of mother who was as likely to find a stray twig tied up in her hair as a fresh packet of extra strong peppermints in her pocket. But she could be a little strict about biscuits.

'I think being friendly would be the nice thing to do,' Mum had nodded, and gone back to studying a scratchy parchment.

As well as being the wisest person Raven knew, one of Mum's amazing qualities was how nice she was to everyone. Her job as a curse breaker meant she spent her days helping misguided sorcerers out of tricky situations. Some could get pretty cross when their magic backfired horribly and she was well practised at looking past the bad in people.

But Mum had not been there on Mortimer Scratch's first day at school, when he had stood by Miss Sunny to say hello. Henry Figgins had chortled and said he thought *Snort*imer was a funny name. An answering snigger had gone around the class.

At first break, Henry had appeared with a bloody nose. When he was being patched up by Mrs Maudlin, the school receptionist and the one who had the enviable responsibility of dishing out all the bandages and plasters from the first aid box, Henry had been strangely quiet about what had happened, mumbling something about having tripped.

So Raven had to find her bravery to screech to a glaring stop right in front of the annoying new boy. Annoying in many ways, not least because he was an extraordinarily good shot. The whispering in Twinhills said the Scratches moved around a lot, mostly to keep their son out of trouble.

'Oh, hello. My name's Mortimer.'

'I know who you are, you're in my class at school,' retorted Raven, concentrating on Mum's advice that if you sound brave, no one knows how you feel inside. How it really felt was as if a little black hole had opened inside her and it was sucking in all her courage. 'What I want to know is why you are squirting water at me.'

He was lean and wiry; taller than Raven, which was true of most people in her class. His hair was dark, possibly even glossier than Rookery's. Raven felt her own name gave an expectation that she should have hair that was dark and straight, like beautiful wings. But that hair had been given to her sister. When she said her name, people tended to repeat it in a certain way – *Raven?* – as if she had somehow got her own name wrong. Because her own hair was annoyingly both fluffy and curly. If anyone had called her after her actual hair she'd have ended up with a name like Alpaca.

The annoying boy had frozen with the water gun in his hand, drops drizzling guiltily from its nozzle. He shifted his arms behind his back, as if that would make the huge, orange water gun invisible. 'What *I* want to know is –' he leant forward and dropped his voice to a whisper – 'how do I meet the witch?'

Raven felt the world spin. This was truly the first time she had ever had to Deny Everything and it gave her a prickling sweatiness that had nothing at all to do with the cycling. A thought had flashed through her mind: he couldn't possibly mean her sister. Could he?

2. THE HOWLING HAG

'You say you want to meet a witch like saying you'd like pickle in your cheese sandwich, Mortimer Scratch.' Raven attempted her best Deny Everything scoff. 'How is that even possible, seeing as witches don't exist?'

Raven told herself to stay calm, to not give away that her stomach felt like rabbits were running around in there. She had been taught from an early age how to respond to Questions. But she could not meet the boy's curious stare, and instead she focused

on a slinky black cat that was basking on top of the inn's sunny wall. It looked half asleep, although its ears were pricked up.

'Can you call me Mort?'

'Why?'

'It's my new name.'

'I don't think I can do that.'

'I don't see why not. Mortimer makes me sound like a nerd.'

'Well, possibly, but I don't want to call you Mort because that just makes you sound dead. Because, you know, it means dead in French? If you ask me, sounding dead is worse than sounding like a nerd.'

'Of course I knew that,' the boy said quickly, though his eyes, which were the colour of autumn conkers, gave him away by opening wider in surprise. 'But not many people are going to know that, are they? You are the smartest person in the class. How about Morti? I'm going to give that a go and see if I like it.'

The cat's green eyes blinked open and then closed again as if to say: *Who is this idiot?* Despite her nerves, it made Raven unexpectedly want to giggle.

'So, how do I find this witch?'

'Why are you asking me?' said Raven stoutly. 'I wouldn't have the faintest idea how to find a witch.

I'm going to see my Grandpa Knox.' She kept her fingers crossed behind her back.

'I didn't mean your grandfather is a witch, that would be stupid,' said Morti.

The cat moved itself into a long stretch and gave another very slow blink, as if saying, *He definitely is an idiot*.

'Is that your cat?' Raven asked.

Morti turned. The black cat had returned to being motionless, except for the tiniest, rhythmic twitch of its tail on the sun-dappled wall. It stared back at Morti, as if this was a staring competition.

'Nah. It hangs around. Guess it must be a stray. Oh no . . . or . . . d'you think it could be the witch's cat spying on us?!'

Raven spluttered. 'Which witch are you *on* about?'

A small hiss came and black fur rose along the cat's back.

'The one they chant about, of course. *She's going to trick you. She's going to get you. She's going to eat you*. Never dare go into Beechy Wood. You're telling me Sam Carruthers would have missed that catch in cricket if he hadn't been cursed by bad luck and burnt his hand? Ella's new shoes vanishing and then reappearing dangling from that spelling trophy?

Thought she'd never stop crying. Don't you want to stop this witch pestering people and being gruesome?'

Raven blinked thoughtfully. So did the black cat. Because, yes, in the last few weeks the school had suffered more than its fair share of unpleasant incidents. Yes, she had heard the playground chanting. She just hadn't paid it much attention.

Morti turned to look along Twinhills' ancient high street, to where the school waited silently until the next day. 'I have never been to a school before that's haunted by some malevolent spirit. And I've moved around a *lot*.'

But there couldn't be a witch. Not one Raven didn't know about. A new witch? One that was trying to curse the school?

Morti pushed open the gate and moved a clanky old bicycle on to the pavement. 'Someone is trying to stop that old witch. Mrs Maudlin found a bottle tied to the front railing. Not just any old bottle – I heard it was full of salt and nails, stuff what witches can't stand. It's called a witch chaser.'

'Witch chaser!' scoffed Raven, getting better at her scoffs now. 'Why would witches not like salt and iron and an old bottle? That's just silly superstition.' But this would not do at all.

12

'This witch is ruining all the fun. I want to stop her and you can help me. We can be like knights.' He straightened the orange basket perched at the front of his bike. 'I'm ready to ride out on my trusty steed.'

On the wind, a low and sarcastic voice seemed to growl: *Trusty steed? Rusty steed more like.*

Raven swung around to look at the cat, because it was almost as if it had spoken out loud.

Raven knew rather more than most people of the rules and power of magic and knew perfectly well that the likelihood of a cat actually being able to talk was very small indeed. She also knew it was incredibly unlikely there were *two* families of witches in Twinhills. The idea was very troubling.

'I'm ready to fight and kill any witches that might be lurking, cackling and doing their fiendish deeds,' said Morti. 'Let's start with your grandfather.'

'Why do you want to start with Grandpa Knox?' spluttered Raven.

'Grandfathers know all the old stories, don't they?' explained Morti. 'We should make like detectives and investigate.'

'I thought we were going to be knights on our rusty steeds— I mean trusty steeds.' She shot another suspicious glance at the cat, who was blinking intelligently as if taking in every word they were saying.

'We'll be witch-hunting detecto-knights.' Morti's face broke into a wide grin that reached his ears.

It was true that Grandpa Knox would know all the old stories about witches. But Raven couldn't take Morti to meet him. There were just too many things he shouldn't see at Dandelion Cottage; Grandpa Knox was terrible at taking secrecy seriously.

Grandma Antirrhinum (luckily everyone only ever called her Snapdragon) had been the cautious one. She had fixed an alert specolens to the kitchen wall, made from a pair of her fanciest sunglasses. You could peer at the lenses and they would show you any unexpected visitors approaching. Snapdragon had been the one to insist that her profession could be dangerous. Yet, sadly, she had been the one to suffer a terrible magical tragedy – one that no one liked to talk about.

Morti and his dreadful bicycle with its dented orange basket were waiting. He pointed up at the awful cackling witch sign hanging outside the inn. 'That's her. The Howling Hag.'

Raven had looked at that sign plenty of times. It showed what people probably thought witches should look like. As if any self-respecting witch would ever go around wearing a pointy hat and riding on a broomstick. That would hardly be secretive, would it? It might just possibly get you noticed. All magic had to be cloaked in absolute secrecy – well, if everyone believed in sorcery, wouldn't everyone want their problems solved by magic?

'The Howling Hag?' Raven winced as she looked at the sign. 'That's who you think is cursing the school?'

She was just about to allow herself a sigh of relief, because *that* witch was not real. But then . . . was there a reason the village inn was called the Howling Hag Inn? There had been strange happenings at school. If she was real, why did Raven not know this?

And what possible reason could she have for cursing the school?

3. Ignoring a Piece of Salmon

Had that boy really called me a *stray*? Stray!

Mortimer Scratch needed to be taught a thing or two about cats.

It is true that humans can be trained. But all that rubbing around the legs, giving them the big old eyes and the purring (they all like the purring) . . . it all takes so much effort. And to be honest, I was here in Twinhills mostly for a holiday. Not to help rude humans like Morti Scratch.

All humans have their faults. Even in very

pleasant houses that are good for a nice piece of salmon and that smell of coffee and freshly swept floors, like the Maudlin family's at the top of Twinhills High Street.

Even there, as I was tidily eating my salmon, they snuck a collar around my neck. I could scarcely believe it. The indignity. It wasn't so much the bell I minded (getting rid of that was the work of a moment). But there was this small circular metal disc with one word on it: *Snoozy*.

That is one of the worst things about humans. The terrible names they give you.

How much easier if you could just come out with it: *It's Nightshade, thank you very much*.

Stray? I would not forget that insult in a hurry.

The troublesome boy, Morti, was awkwardly holding out a packet of prawn cocktail crisps as he tried to manoeuvre his awful bike on to the street. Raven, a bright and considerate child, reached out to help him and looked thoughtful as she accepted the crisps.

'I can tell that you are annoying mostly because it's the way to be noticed and you want to make new friends,' she said. 'But that you are really very kind, you always mean well and are warm and generous.' Higher praise than he deserved.

I could see Raven Charming was dithering over the seriously bad idea of taking him to Knox's. Did she really need me to leap in and point out the dangers? Not a danger that Morti might find himself zapped and suddenly sprout white fur and whiskers (the Charmings were skilful enough for that not to happen). But there are things the eyes of a nosy boy like Morti Scratch are not supposed to see.

'I knew you were smart, that is totally how it is!' nodded Morti. 'Is that witchcraft? Bet you know I stole these crisps too. But no one'll miss them.' He shook out some more into her hand. 'These prawn cocktails are dead unpopular.'

They chatted, I listened: Raven stoutly denying anything to do with witchcraft was real, Morti pointing out some of the unsettling things that had started happening at the school. Like that chanting. And he might be right.

I'd heard it. It went around like a scared whisper after anything strange happened. *She's going to trick you. She's going to get you. She's going to eat you.* Not something you want to hear in any school. And I'd started to watch Rookery Charming, standing to one side of the crowd, watching the latest incident unfold with her creepily intense light-brown, sometimes yellow eyes.

There can be trouble when you are young and not fully trained in the magical arts. Sometimes you do magic without even meaning to. Can lead to uncomfortable questions if someone notices. It was certainly going to be pretty awkward for Rookery Charming if there really were two witches in Twinhills and one of them was up to no good.

I shrugged myself up and padded along the warm wall, dappled with nice end-of-afternoon sunlight, and reminded myself I was on holiday. All I wanted to care about was that it was almost time for a nice plump fillet of salmon to be dropped into a nice clean china bowl at the Maudlins'.

'Even cycling up that hill is better than staying here,' said Morti, glancing at a house which stood to attention between the school and the inn. It was called Tidy House and, true to its name, it had a garden so neat that weeds would not dare drop their seeds on it. 'Don't want to risk being here and having to watch Mr Odorless spray weedkiller all over again.'

That was indeed one of the most unfortunate things about the very pleasant village of Twinhills – the head teacher lived right next door to the school. And Mr Odorless himself was unfortunate. He had a pale, very flat face, although this could turn a nasty shade of violet when he was cross. Which, as far as I could tell, was most of the time.

I was actually waiting for him to arrive as it brought me a fun moment in my day: Titus would be let into the garden. An objectionable, small, yappy, snappy excuse for a pooch. Utterly hideous. When I lay full stretch along the top of this wall, my tail can't help being the perfect length – it dangles slightly higher than Titus is able to jump. Annoys him into a snapping, wheezing frenzy. Quite irresistible joy.

So much better than a hot walk trying to prevent a couple of kids from plunging headlong into some very nasty trouble, or worse – some seriously sinister magic.

I heard the sound of the front door of the school being locked, followed by the familiar tread of Mr Odorless's scuttling footsteps as his short figure approached. I think that sound made Raven decide. Because she and Morti began the tough cycle up the very tediously long hill to Knox's, presumably with a plan to tackle bad magic and possibly upset a vengeful witch, as if that would be no trickier than sharpening your claws on a tree.

The end of my tail twitched in readiness at a delightful few moments tormenting Titus, followed by a superb piece of plump fresh salmon. Then a comfy cushion right where the afternoon sun would have moved to. My definition of a perfect afternoon.

But I was getting that feeling. The one I get when a mouse I've been watching silently, intently, and without moving for a very long time, thinks I've gone. That feeling that nothing good was going to happen.

Was I really going to give up my holiday and help that insulting boy?

Stray!

Surely there was no choice. I leapt off the sunny wall and trotted along after them.

4. AN UPROAR OF UNTIDINESS

I took the cross-country route through the dark and shady heart of Beechy Wood. It didn't stop it feeling like the wrong day to be wearing fur, and Morti and Raven still arrived ahead of me.

Most people would pass by and not even notice Dandelion Cottage. The cottage was wound with long tendrils of protective ivy and stitched together with moss and appeared to grow out of the wood itself. Daisies sprouted on its grass roof. You had to look closely to see the jumble of logs entwined with

leaves and branches for what it really was. But perhaps that was the point.

I finally flopped up at my destination and slumped, practically melting on to the nice wide windowsill, peering into the kitchen, hoping someone would notice me and bring out a nice refreshing drink. Raven and Morti were torturing me with a lot of slurping and loud rattling of ice cubes as they sipped tall glasses of home-made lemonade. I pressed my pink nose against the glass.

Dandelion Cottage must be heaven for one of those can-never-be-still children like Morti. He pushed at a jar marked *spaghetti* here, closed a drawer full of string there, all the while explaining the unpleasant incidents at school to a man with luxuriantly long and dark curly hair who busily spooned dollops of red jam into pastry cases. Knox Charming.

What I'd seen of Knox in the short time I'd been in Twinhills told me he was very much the sort who could do a spell to lock a door, but he wasn't likely to remember to use it.

At least there was one thing he was careful about – he kept the secret trapdoor to where he did his spells hidden. A fancy patterned rug disguised it completely. All magical folk tend to be pretty good at keeping magic a secret. Yet Morti Scratch had only just arrived in Twinhills for the last term of the year and he had latched right on to the fact that there were witches here. This was not good.

'It's small things mostly, but strange,' Morti was explaining, while slurping noisily. 'Ones that upset people. Like Ella got these fancy red shoes that totally vanished. They reappeared magically dangling either side of the spelling trophy on the shelf outside the school office. Gave everyone a laugh – 'cept Ella, of course.'

My detective instincts were twitching. If Morti Scratch was right, this Howling Hag was going to ruin things for a lot of people. Not least these two, if they seriously planned on tackling a sorcerer who sounded as if she was bent on mischief. How was that going to end – other than with one of them on the pointy end of a very nasty spell?

'Money was swiped and there was some mystery about how it was taken. Miss Percy went around looking grim for days. We lost to Fivetors *again* because of Sam Carruthers – you can't tell me it was just bad luck he burnt his hand and fumbled a catch in cricket *and* lost the tennis tournament to Bianca in the same week. You can't tell me this isn't a dangerous curse we're up against. Old Odorless was mad as a hornet in a jar when Sam missed that catch.'

Knox made a slightly strangled response. 'I know Twinhills is riddled with superstition, but what makes you think any of that was down to a witch?'

'It's the chanting, mostly.' Morti shuddered. 'Then there's those words that appeared on the board in Miss Sunny's classroom: *Watch out! I am here and I am going to eat you.*'

'I can see how that might upset people,' said Knox as he began delving distractedly through an assortment of canisters lined on a crowded dresser before eventually finding one marked *tea*. When he lifted the lid, he looked puzzled as he extracted a handful of miniature scrolls made from ancient paper.

'But that message on the board was just a joke, wasn't it?' put in Raven, slurping the last of her lemonade.

I settled down, interested to hear how Knox was going to deal with a load of very intrusive questions. Because you could not ignore that people here were more than a little jumpy, as if an ill wind had blown in from Beechy Wood.

Knox stuck his thumbs into his plum-coloured waistcoat. I had yet to see him without a velvet waistcoat and matching bow tie, as if he hung around awaiting invitations to important places, even when sliding a tray of jam tarts into the oven like he'd just done. Did the man even possess any pyjamas?

Knox slowly made a brew in a large striped mug and asked mildly if Morti would even know if he met a witch. This was an impossible question, one that tested the minds of some of the most senior Elysee sorcerers: How can you tell if someone is magical? Morti Scratch had no idea what he might be up against.

'Course! I'd spot one right off,' answered Morti quickly. 'They wear gloves, as they have claws instead of fingers. They have a secret plan to take over the world by turning children into mice by offering them sweets.'

Knox lifted the lid of a jar marked *coffee*. He took out a white paper bag and held it out to Morti, who extracted a chocolate rabbit and bit off the head cleanly.

'They use crystal balls to check out what ill will befall you.' Morti hardly paused to nibble the feet of the chocolate rabbit. 'They make straw dolls and stick pins in to make you do stuff. If you don't avoid their evil eye they make you sick just by looking at you. They feed you potions, bad spells they've made in big black bubbling cauldrons full of disgusting stuff while muttering evil enchantments they've found in crusty old spell books.'

Knox lifted an ancient book from the centre of the kitchen table and tidied it on to a shelf. 'Always women, are they? Men don't make the grade?' He offered another round of chocolate rabbits and lounged against the stove, where an enormous black saucepan simmered gently.

'And I suppose they have pet toads and cats,' put in Raven Charming with a nice scoff. 'And cackle, wear pointy hats and fly around on broomsticks.'

Morti bit off a second rabbit head. 'They curse your sheep, sour the milk. And they make your crops fail.'

'I'm not so sure all that many people these days have sheep and crops to worry about.' Knox tucked away a stray scroll inside a jar marked *sugar* and sipped his tea. He sniffed the air suspiciously, as if trying to remember if he was in the middle of doing something.

I hoped he was going to recognize the smell of jam tarts browning nicely.

Morti lifted the lid on a butter dish and leapt back, startled, as a soft brown toad crawled out. 'Oh. Does this belong to anyone?'

'Ah, Mimi!' said Knox. 'I wondered where she was.' He gathered the toad to him and plopped her out on the front doorstep. If a toad can look affronted, that was how Mimi looked as she crawled into a hole in a big stone. 'She croaks to me every morning and has the most beautiful voice.'

Morti was continuing unstoppably. 'They have huge nostrils to sniff out children to eat them. Worst thing you can do is be clean as you give off the most ghastly stench to a witch. I reckon all the kids at Twinhills should stop taking baths immediately.'

'Um, I think you might find,' said Knox, fiddling with his bow tie, 'that at least part of that is from a book by Roald Dahl. It is a very good book, but that doesn't make it true.'

He dragged a hand through his perfect hair and leant on the rough bark of the tree that grew through the centre of the cottage.

Most magical folk are not trying to eat children, let alone try to take over the world. Most magical people I know are too busy practising getting a door to slam or bending a spoon. Magic can be a proper pain to get right. It's one of the reasons magic needs to remain a secret. Because if it got out about magic you can bet people would go around demanding miracles for breakfast. People tend to assume magic can do a lot more than it really does. It would bring a lot of expectation and lead to a lot of disappointment. And it would mean trouble for all those magical folk pottering about their daily business, using their magic quietly to help people, in the way that all magical folk should.

'Occasionally people might call on a wise woman,' said Knox carefully. 'They used to be called "cunning folk", and they were once an accepted part of village life. Skill with herbs and a few well-chosen words can—'

'What we need to know is the best way to tackle the Howling Hag and stop her being mean to everyone. That witch bottle tied to the front of the school isn't going to cut it.'

Knox blinked at Morti's interruption. 'The Howling Hag? Who's the Howling Hag?'

'There's a picture of her on the sign outside my new home,' Morti pointed out helpfully. 'I heard there's a legend and my dad was decorating and found these weird symbols carved into the woodwork. You can come and see them if you like. The inn is dead old. Dad looked 'em up and them symbols are to ward off evil. Same as that witch bottle. Anyway, it has to be an evil witch targeting the school, because of that black cat. It's been hanging around, poking its pink nose into everything. It's a sign. Worse is about to happen.'

This jolted me out of my almost-snooze. Hanging around and poking in a pink nose? I had a nasty feeling the boy might be talking about me.

I have been keeping watch. It's easy to do. Well, it is if you're a cat. The teachers have been delighted that such a very smart and dignified cat should choose to keep an eye on the place. Pretty much all the children are lovely, as long as they keep away from my fur. Their hands, particularly the youngest of them, are a little sticky, often covered in paint, glue, or a smear of whatever was in their sandwich for lunch.

'*Tarts!*' Finally Knox launched a rescue mission, using a pair of oven gloves shaped like goldfish, sliding the pastries on to the big table in the centre of the kitchen, jam still bubbling.

'Witches have black cats, that's something *everyone* knows,' insisted Morti. 'That black cat hanging around has to be the Howling Hag's. Probably marking out the next victim.'

'Next victim?' echoed Knox, hunting about for plates and finding some under a pile of freshly picked herbs.

I hadn't come to Twinhills to save a cursed school. Or to track down witches or save annoying boys. I was here because there had been no place for me in the latest adventure of my best friend and partner in crime, Seth Seppi. He was undercover on a case for MagiCon, the magical police. An old friend of his father's lived hereabouts and I deserved a break. I was glad to be away from all the skulduggery and exhausting mayhem that generally surrounds Seth. My life has more explosions and showdowns with sorcerers-gone-bad than is usual for most cats. It interferes with both snoozetimes and mealtimes. Despite all that – call it super detective senses if you like – I'd drifted into watching the school. But I didn't want my holiday to be over.

I did quite want a jam tart.

It would be the work of a moment to get to that table. I could swipe a tart and be out of here before anyone even noticed.

I moved from the window ledge, silent as a shadow, sneaked along to the door and slipped inside. I leapt beautifully, with all my natural grace, landing on all four paws perfectly and soundlessly on the kitchen table, right next to where a dozen tarts had been placed to cool.

I reached out a paw gently to seize one. But it was at just that moment that Morti Scratch, the bothersome boy who had not stopped pacing and sticking his nose into everything, made the same decision.

The whole tray was precariously balanced, and as we both went for it at the same moment, the whole lot tipped. There was a clatter and a dozen perfect tarts cascaded into a crumbly sticky heap on the kitchen floor.

There are many important things you learn when you are a cat – including how and when to make a hasty exit. And how to make sure you never have to clear up after yourself.

5. DEFINITELY NOT DOING MAGIC

Morti Scratch had gone on about that cat being the Howling Hag's spy, deliberately upsetting those tarts to stop him finding out any more from Grandpa Knox. But Raven had more urgent things on her mind than his insistence that the unpleasantness at school had to mean a malevolent witch was at work.

Every spare moment of the past couple of days, Raven had been tidying and disguising the magical clutter of their home. Because the risk of discovery

of the Charmings' magical lifestyle was all too real and happening right now – danger was going to step right through their door.

Rookery had a friend coming to tea.

Rookery was not quite two years older than Raven, with their birthdays falling at opposite ends of the year. And they were opposites in so many ways. Rookery seemed to be growing taller than she needed to be and Raven felt she would never catch her up.

Rookery was silent and still as a lake. There was something more than a little unnerving about the way she looked at you, as if she could peer deep inside and know what you were thinking. She had midnight-dark hair that made the rest of her look like it was made of moonlight. Raven pretty much felt that Rookery was always just a step away from having to Deny Everything.

Raven, on the other hand, longed for any signs of being magical at all.

At first, Mum had decided against sending them just along the road to Twinhills School and they had gone every day to the neighbouring town, to Fivetors School. Mum no doubt hoped in a big school like Fivetors there was less chance of people noticing if anything strange happened around

Rookery. Raven understood how much her sister needed to be protected from anyone discovering her secret. Rookery was so very magical, it was difficult for her to stop it spilling out sometimes. Often, Rookery explained, magic just happened.

Not going to Twinhills School had meant that neither Raven nor Rookery ever got invited to the village parties. But they heard about them. Bianca Maudlin threw the biggest ones. 'Show-offy parties,' Rookery always said, before she'd finally been invited.

Just after Christmas, Mum had unexpectedly switched the girls to Twinhills. It wasn't the first time they'd had to make a quick change, like Rookery's table tennis classes ending, just when tongues started to wag at the way Rookery could reach even the fastest and trickiest shots.

Even so, it was difficult to understand. Twinhills was so small there was a high chance of people noticing if things happened when Rookery was around. At Twinhills, there weren't even enough numbers to make up whole classes; the years were all jumbled up, younger ones mostly shuffled into Miss Sunny's class and the older ones being taught by Miss Percy.

But at least the move to the local village school

meant Rookery had finally been invited to one of Bianca's famous parties.

And all the rumours were true. Bianca had a whole miniature zoo set up in her back garden, just for the party. Stick insects you could watch in case they did anything; tiny, mini ponies you could give an apple to. And there were rabbits. Rookery had been rather desperate to be invited to Bianca's next party. 'There might be rabbits again,' she'd said excitedly.

So Raven had set about not minding when Rookery started walking with Bianca after school, or going to see her guinea pigs rather than wanting to head into Beechy Wood to the sisters' den that was waiting for their return; or climbing trees, swinging on branches, making daisy chains and laughing at scampering squirrels.

But Rookery having a best friend brought a whole new danger. Raven had taken a deep, nervous breath when she'd heard Rookery pleading with Mum to invite her new friend to tea.

Finch had removed her glasses and fished around in her pockets for one of her extra-strong mints. 'I shall cook a special dinner.'

'No!' Rookery had responded quickly. 'I'll ask Dad.'

At Bianca's they had been served dainty sandwiches, crusts removed, on colourful plates alongside scones with jam, cream and butter (Rookery hadn't known which to choose, so she had simply helped herself to all three) and four different types of cake. Four.

But Dad had to go abroad to a conference talking about making better roads with fewer holes. Dad said how much easier it would be if everyone could simply dash around on broomsticks. Dad always remained remarkably calm about being swept into the magic of the Charming family, even though he wasn't the slightest bit magical. And Dad definitely did much better dinners than Mum.

'We'll have pie. It'll be fine,' Mum had announced, in a voice that had sounded far more confident than either of the girls felt.

Raven had shared a look with her sister, thinking casserole, or possibly pasta, as these were their two favourite dishes of those Finch cooked. As far as Raven knew, they were the only two dishes Mum could make. She guessed they would just have to wait and see exactly what pie the future brought.

If only the biggest problem was going to be the pie.

The stress of taking the inquisitive Morti up to

Grandpa Knox's had highlighted the danger of a pair of sharp eyes and eager questions. Mum was as bad as Grandpa Knox. She left half-done spells everywhere, even at the same time as warning Rookery and Raven of the importance of tidying away all evidence of their family's magic into the secret room all witches had beneath the floorboards or behind a chimney.

Raven loved being admitted to the inner, secret world of sorcerers; loved the fact that one of the Charmings' bookcases revolved to reveal a secret chamber behind the chimney stack. She enjoyed her studies, learning what happened in the Elysee, the organization that ran the magical world; hearing of the lives of enchanters and healers, wise women and seers, of magic used for good and evil.

She'd first learnt of magic when she noticed the biggest and tastiest cakes moving to her sister's side of the plate so she could 'politely' take the one nearest. Then Raven had waited excitedly to see what form her own magic would take.

Right now she should be sitting down with Mum and a pile of thick, well-thumbed ancient books, going over a whole load of subjects that partly confused and terrified her. Yet she loved her magical lessons, looking through the books and speculating what her magical affinity would be.

Instead, right now she was dusting her hands after a lot of tidying, feeling confident, at least, that a toad was not going to crawl out from under the butter dish.

Just in time. There was a noise from the garden door that led on to the busy shortcut up to the top of the village, and Rookery crept in with Bianca.

'Bianca, welcome!' said Mum, overdoing it and totally giving away that having friends around was very far from normal.

Bianca was always glamorous, even at school. Probably because of her fabulously silky, long and enviably straight hair. Today she was wearing a fashionable short skirt and had a red sparkly handbag that matched a hairband that was keeping her locks perfect.

Raven had minded less about Rookery becoming best friends with Bianca when Mum had said she was old enough now to cycle to Grandpa Knox's on her own. You never knew what might be happening at Dandelion Cottage, but Raven felt sure it was more exciting than anything that might happen at Bianca's. Bianca lived in the biggest house in Twin-hills – all grand and symmetrical and slightly aloof at the top of the village. It looked down on to the middle of the village and the two narrow rows of weathered-stone cottages that slouched against each other like a shabby family down on their luck.

From the way Bianca's gaze instantly began to move with undisguised curiosity around the jumbled, colourful inside of Sundial Cottage, Raven could guess she wasn't used to a home where the sofas sagged quite so comfortably. Even Raven was embarrassed by the terrible cushions with pictures of sad kittens. Grandma Snapdragon had made them for Mum one Christmas during a thankfully short-lived passion for tapestry.

Mum offered Bianca a cup of tea.

Rookery nervously said that Bianca didn't like tea, so Mum offered some of Knox's home-made lemonade instead as Raven hurriedly tucked away a spell scroll that had rolled out from under the desk. Bianca said she preferred apple juice.

Mum had put on tight jeans, rather than the flowing skirt she usually wore. The skirt looked like it had been made from cobwebs and was full of magical pockets from where she could produce almost anything, from an extra-strong mint if she needed to think, to a chunk of chocolate if you scraped your knee, or *Two Hundred Favourite Charms to Help Around the Home*, which was the book she dipped into when she was in a hurry and there was a pile of washing that wasn't going to clean itself.

Mum really was on her best behaviour. She had even tied up her hair with something other than a twig. It looked like she'd chosen something plastic and colourful, probably found in Rookery's bedroom. Honestly, Raven thought a twig looked better.

Instead of apologizing for the lack of any apple juice, Mum drifted off to sit at her big desk, staring into the distance and chewing on the end of her glasses. She frowned at the empty space where one of her spell parchments would normally be, as if her mind was still on the case of the transforming silver. She stirred her mug with a green goose quill and then suddenly twirled it.

And when Rookery opened the fridge, the lemonade in the jug was suddenly apple juice. Raven had been trying to catch Mum's eye and remind her: *Dinner!* But now she stared open-mouthed. *Mum!* Who was always warning of the dire consequences if any magical person broke the Golden Rule of openly doing magic?

Bianca was politely asking about biscuits and Rookery was taking down the Little Miss Organized tin. She started to prise off the lid, just as Bianca said: 'We always have chocolate ones at home.'

And suddenly the tin was crammed with three different kinds of chocolate biscuits. Mum refused to meet the eyes of the two girls. Because that tin only ever contained healthy oat-based snacks that Dad made at the weekends, heavy with lots of nuts and seeds.

Bianca took a bite of chocolate biscuit and closed her eyes. 'Mmmm. Nicer than the ones we have at home.'

Mum began whistling very off-tune and got up to go to the window and opened it, muttering something about it being hot.

Raven sneaked another biscuit. She could get to like having people for tea.

But her good feeling lasted seconds. Because Bianca was wandering towards one of the bookcases, her eye on something Raven had completely missed. The magical seeing crystal, lying there on a shelf, with Bianca's hand just centimetres away.

6. How Not To Bake A Pie

'Rookery said you have lots of pets,' squeaked Raven, flying forward to seize the crystal that predicted the future. Well, Rookery was the only one who could get it to foretell anything. She looked into it occasionally to see if Dad was being optimistic when he said tea would be ready in five minutes. It was pretty rubbish really. 'Rookery said she met your new hamster yesterday.'

'He's the fluffiest hamster I've ever seen,' sighed Rookery in a voice that made it clear that hamster

was going to be very spoilt.

Bianca's curious eyes were drinking in everything with an obvious thirst to find out about the Charmings. Raven hoped the only stories Bianca would have to tell were of the chipped teapot and Mum's wobbly desk propped up by a pile of books. She swooped in with another distracting chocolate biscuit, but could almost feel the curiosity burning off Bianca.

Raven's heart was hammering – it had already had enough of living dangerously. She wished Rookery would take Bianca upstairs to show her her room. How much easier life would be if they could just live among people who knew about magic.

Bianca veered off towards another bookcase which Raven and Rookery had crammed with all the most boring and ordinary books they had been able to find. The crystal seemed forgotten for now, and Raven released the breath she had been holding.

'What's your new hamster called?' she asked, hopping from one leg to the other.

'Lady McFluff,' replied Bianca. 'Mum says it's a rotten name.'

'Bianca is really good with names. Didn't your mum want you to call him Captain Fluffball?' said Rookery.

'Yes, because he's a boy hamster. But I wanted a girl hamster and anyway, how can you tell? No one's going to know, are they? Mum is so rubbish at names. She once had a bird she called Little Miss Tweets who then lost her voice and couldn't tweet at all.'

There was a noise, a swoosh from where Mum had opened the window in the kitchen. A black cat came slinking through. That same black cat – it had been sitting on the wall outside the Howling Hag Inn and had then arrived unexpectedly at Knox's and destroyed all those jam tarts. Morti had said this was the Howling Hag's cat and that it was spying. And now it was here. It felt a little as if it really *was* spying.

'It's Snoozy!' cried Bianca. 'She must have followed me here.'

The cat jumped on the floor and began to rub around Rookery's legs.

Rookery immediately crouched down to pet her and picked her up. 'Lucky you to have such a gorgeous cat.' The cat purred deeply. 'What very soft fur. And she's called Snoozy?'

The cat stopped purring and opened her big green eyes wide.

'We didn't buy Snoozy,' admitted Bianca, tickling the cat in Rookery's arms. 'But Snoozy likes our house the best and calls in every day at teatime. She only eats salmon.'

And jam tarts, Raven wanted to say.

'Some people think black cats are awfully unlucky,' said Bianca. 'Mum took in a black cat once, Mick, who took everyone by surprise by having seven kittens.'

'Yes, that does sound unlucky,' said Mum, looking up from where she was lost in her own thoughts, fiddling with her silver bracelet studded with seven different coloured jewels. It was a device that helped detect when magic had been used.

'Dad went completely bonkers with them going wild and climbing the curtains,' Bianca went on. 'So Mum knocked on every door pleading with people to take one. Mum got a job at the school soon after. Said looking after all those children was a whole lot easier than kittens.'

'When is dinner?' Rookery asked, pointedly looking at Mum, who was lost in thought, watching the cat. 'I'm starving.'

It didn't need the seeing crystal to reveal Mum had forgotten all about a pie.

'Dinner!' Finch scrambled out from behind her desk. She made for the kitchen, removing her rings and bracelet as she hunted for a cookery book and flour.

The black cat made a dash for the stairs and Raven suggested quickly that Rookery follow and take Bianca upstairs to her room. Finally, she relaxed. She took out *A Short History of Some Most Interesting and Remarkable Magical Folk* from where she had hidden it behind one of the awful embroidered cushions. Usually, this time every week, Mum would twirl her magical bracelet and help Raven with her studies. Raven never wanted to waste time with Mum on the kind of tedious questions the teachers were so bothered about. Was there an easier way of doing long division? How many r's were in harassment? Or why, when you mixed all the colours in your paint tray, instead of a beautiful rainbow, you ended up with something that looked like it had been dug from the bottom of the school pond?

Raven wanted to concentrate every moment on the good stuff. The magic.

With Bianca here, Mum wouldn't be able to go through Raven's questions and today, she was keen to learn what Mum might know about this other local witch. Mum was scattering flour liberally over random surfaces, squinting at a recipe and cutting butter with the same worried and determined look on her face as when she was trying to unpick a love potion that had been drunk by the wrong person.

Raven flicked though the book, half watching Mum roll out pastry like she was slapping together mud pies. Raven hoped Mum's ability to bake a pie would be even half as good as her ability to break a curse.

At first, Raven thought she might like to be a seer. Being able to take a peek into the future seemed an attractive idea, but she had quickly worked out that would completely ruin things like birthday surprises.

Lately her questions had started changing.

Part of her still had the heart to ask: *When will my affinity arrive?* But slowly, what had begun to worry her more was: *What will I do if I have no magic?*

When Grandma Snapdragon had her accident, and Snapdragon was no more, a little hole of fear had opened inside of Raven and had been growing. That tiny, secret fear was making itself heard louder and louder and it told her magic was dangerous. It gave her a new question. *Do you even want to be a sorcerer after what happened to Snapdragon?*

Raven eventually closed the book. She hadn't found a single mention of the Howling Hag. Was there any point in her reading these books? What was the point in learning about magic if she didn't have any magic?

The pie was in the oven and Mum was back at her desk.

'Mum, what can you tell me about the Howling Hag? I didn't know there was another local witch.'

'Local witch? Oh, you needn't worry,' Mum smiled distractedly. 'There's only one magical family in Twinhills.' Mum's answer was spectacularly unhelpful, although that might be because she kept glancing anxiously at the oven as if anticipating something going wrong.

Laughter drifted from upstairs. Raven listened to the giggling and could hear chatter about the possibility of Rookery getting a pet. She was glad her sister had a best friend. Even though, for all her life, Raven had been the one Rookery whispered to. Part of that, Raven knew, was because of the big secret they shared. It was easier not to have friends when you had so many things to keep secret.

Quite a lot later, Rookery called downstairs, 'Mum! Bianca and I are really hungry, when is dinner?'

Finch gave a worried glance at the oven. There was still no delicious smell. She went and carefully opened it and began to chew her bottom lip and stared at a pie, which had not even started to cook.

'Oh, racoons! I was so worried I'd burn it, I forgot to switch the oven on at all,' she said in a low voice.

Finch took a hasty glance over her shoulder. But Bianca had remained safely upstairs. Very quietly, Raven heard her murmur a chant over the pie and instantly it became crisp and golden and there was a heavenly smell. Even the potatoes, abandoned in a saucepan, roasted themselves and turned crisp and golden.

Mum gave a guilty complicit smile at Raven and called: 'Dinner's ready, girls!'

Magic might sometimes make life incredibly difficult, but most of the time it was utterly wonderful. If only Raven's magic would finally arrive. And be something useful and not at all scary.

7. The Death of Mr Pickles

Everyone adored Miss Sunny. And everyone loved Mr Pickles, the class mascot, who lived on a top shelf among Miss Sunny's clutter of broken tiles for mosaics, a collection of Roman soldiers and a cardboard model of a villa.

It was a bit of a treat if Mr Pickles joined in when someone had done something good. But a tremor of quiet nervousness rippled around the class if anyone had done something bad. Even the oldest kids in the class who reckoned they were far too grown up,

couldn't quite sneer whenever Miss Sunny tipped her head on one side and said, 'Mr Pickles has someone he wants to speak to.'

And everyone wondered if Mr Pickles would be speaking in his happy voice.

There was heated school debate about exactly what Mr Pickles was. Miss Sunny said her grandmother had knitted him from white wool and no one liked to be rude and say she hadn't exactly done the best job.

He had a long nose and whiskers made out of black wool. But he was about the size of a hot water bottle, which was quite wrong if he was supposed to be a mouse. So some claimed Mr Pickles was really a wolf disguised as a mouse.

There were always nervous giggles when Miss Sunny brought down Mr Pickles and pretended he was looking around the class. The best was when Mr Pickles spoke in his happy and squeaky voice: 'Mr Pickles is very pleased with someone today.' And someone was about to be chosen. Everyone did know it was just Miss Sunny putting on the voice, but it was a bit of a laugh, and sometimes Mr Pickles sat at your table for the rest of the day. It was a thrill to be chosen, even if you pretended you were too cool to care.

But if someone had been a bit rude or disruptive, eyes would gradually shift in their direction. Because it was deeply traumatic if you got Mr Pickles's low and disappointed voice, as he told someone he would be keeping a special Mr Pickles eye on them. The shame tended to follow you the rest of the day.

Mr Pickles wore a blue peaked cap with the words 'I ♥ Cheese' and a smart pair of red-striped bloomers with lace trim around the bottom. These had been donated by Bianca Maudlin after several incidents where Mr Pickles had spoken to her in his disappointed voice.

Mr Pickles was fun and he was adored, even by those who had moved on into Miss Percy's class. But then Twinhills School really did need something to make up for the bad stuff, which was mostly Mr Odorless. Sometimes Raven thought the main job of old Odorless was to deflate as much joy and fun out of the day as possible.

It was the last day of a really hot week at school and Raven had been finding it difficult to stay awake in the hot and sticky classroom when she realized Mr Pickles was being brought down from his shelf to praise Misha's reading. Misha did not like reading and particularly not reading aloud. But he had just got through a whole paragraph with hardly a stutter and Mr Pickles was telling him in his squeaky voice how proud he'd made Mr Pickles and Misha was giggling, when Mr Odorless walked in, taking a sip of coffee from his 'World's Best Head Teacher' mug that everyone knew he must have bought himself. The whole jolly atmosphere in the room changed.

Mr Odorless scuttled in on his short legs and said something in a low voice to Miss Sunny. She was still holding Mr Pickles and her face took on a worried look.

'You are lucky, because Mr Odorless is going to spend some time with you while I just pop to the office for a minute,' announced Miss Sunny. 'Perhaps you'd like to carry on with our story,' she suggested, with a smile at the head teacher.

He placed his mug on her desk and perched alongside it. 'Well, Miss Sunny's class. This year's Miss Percy's class are our best for years and I'm expecting you to work even harder, because you must do even better when your turn comes and it will be sooner than you think. This year we will beat Fivetors in our end of year exams. First time in twelve years! Won't that be something to celebrate! We will show that head teacher Miss Earnest, won't we? So, would you prefer a spelling test or times tables? You can never have too many times tables practices, can you?' He rubbed his pale hands together.

But a voice piped up. 'But we've just reached a very exciting part of the story and we'd all love to hear you read for us.'

Everyone turned, because it had been Mr Pickles' voice.

Miss Sunny was still carrying him as she headed for the door. And he was using his disappointed voice on Mr Odorless!

Mr Odorless blinked and his face turned a twinge of pink. He said nothing. He did not even turn to look at Miss Sunny or Mr Pickles. He took the open book on Miss Sunny's desk and everyone shuffled their bottoms on their chairs and waited to hear what was going to happen to all the dogs trapped in the coal cellar with the baddies who wanted their skins lurking evilly outside.

And Mr Odorless closed the book and pushed it away.

And a small voice could be heard saying: 'Mr Pickles is very disappointed,' just as Miss Sunny left the classroom. And the door closed behind her and the whole class burst into a wave of delighted laughter.

Except Mr Odorless. He had a pale face, but it was a face that went from colourless to red and then purple in a second. And it went very purple indeed.

'Who can tell me how to spell caustic?' said Mr Odorless, a blue vein pulsing on his forehead. And before any of the good spellers had a chance to put up their hand, he turned to Misha. 'Misha, spell caustic and put it in a sentence.'

Misha didn't even have the courage to shake his head.

Miss Sunny said that she believed school was a good place to learn many things. Like the importance of being kind. How to work with people who might be slower than you at understanding their sums, and to see the good in everyone.

Raven only ever heard Mr Odorless muttering that what was important was beating Fivetors at something, anything. And he always got them practising times tables, because he said reading was a waste of time when you could be getting quicker at working out seven times nine.

It was after lunch that Miss Sunny noticed Mr Pickles was no longer in his usual place watching over her class. She knew she had put him back safely and a search began. Miss Percy's class joined in.

The two teachers lived together in a cosy cottage right on Twinhills High Street, not far along from the Hag. It was always easy to imagine them sitting together of an evening eating buttered toast and sipping big mugs of tea and discussing how incredibly straight the Romans had made the roads and why Henry VIII had ended up quite so wicked.

No one owned up to having moved Mr Pickles. Once Miss Sunny was sure Mr Pickles was nowhere in the classroom, the search became more desperate. It started out like a giant game of hide and seek but grew frenzied as it became clear Mr Pickles had completely disappeared.

At the end of second break, Mr Pickles still had not been found, but the game, now started, seemed to take on an unstoppable life of its own.

Mr Odorless hurried out from where he spent most of the day lurking in his office, drinking all the best coffee so he didn't have to share with the other staff. His face was already pink with rage and turning purple as his short steps scuttled him towards where Miss Percy and Miss Sunny were talking anxiously in a corner, while the whole school failed to head back into their classrooms.

'What is the meaning of this? How are our children going to beat Fivetors if we don't get them into a classroom and sat at their desks?'

Mr Odorless's fists tightened and he moved even

closer to the two teachers, aiming for Miss Sunny, because Miss Percy was a good few centimetres taller than Mr Odorless, plus she led them on all the outdoors walks and was a black belt in three different martial arts.

'The children are worried and I think they might find it difficult to concentrate right now,' answered Miss Sunny mildly.

If Raven had been even the tiniest bit brave, one day she would put up her hand and ask Mr Odorless why he ever became a teacher when he seemed to hate teaching only just a little more than he hated children. It was a bit like opening a sweet shop despite being disappointed if people ate your sweets because you felt really they should be eating cabbage instead.

She looked carefully at his face. Did Mr Odorless look guilty? She wanted to ask him if he had slipped into Miss Sunny's classroom himself after Mr Pickles had made everyone laugh at him.

But there came a loud cry.

'Found him! He's here! Miss, he's here!'

And the whole school clustered to follow the jubilant cheers to the school pond, a shallow muddy puddle, fenced-off so none of the smaller children accidentally fell in. It was full of things that swam or sank down to the slurpy bottom, which was lovely and soupy to poke with a long stick, with black mud so thick it stayed on the end. The odd frog would randomly plop out and make you jump.

Mr Pickles was face down in the mud, without his blue 'I ♥ Cheese' cap, his white fur streaked and matted. Before anyone could chirp in with an optimistic *he just needs a nice wash*, Miss Percy, who had stepped right into the pond to haul him out, turned him over.

There was a collective gasp from the whole school.

And that was the moment Raven knew Morti was right: bad things were happening. Someone was cursing the school.

This time Raven heard it as clear as anything. The chanting began, first low and barely above a whisper and then clear and loud: *She's going to trick you. She's going to get you. She's going to eat you.*

It was plain for everyone to see that Mr Pickles had not simply mysteriously fallen into the water, a long way from his proud home high on the top shelf. Mr Pickles hadn't just lost his 'I ♥ Cheese' cap and gotten a bit soggy and muddy. Mr Pickles had come to an unfortunate, messy and very final end.

Mr Pickles had a big pair of scissors lodged right in the middle of his red-striped bloomers.

8. The Secret Signal

Mum was up against it with a puzzling curse to crack. Someone had tried to cheat by cleaning a whole load of valuable family silver with a magical enchantment. Now all their spoons and candlesticks were made of chocolate.

Sometimes the cases Finch Charming was called out on were dangerous. Sometimes she'd go to high-level, top-secret magical discussions about sorcerers who had gone bad, or disappear on long journeys to gather magical plants from far-off places to help

crack the most unbreakable of curses.

But right now she was walking Rookery up to her Saturday morning ballet lesson in Twinhills Village Hall.

Raven took her chance to dive into *One Hundred of the Deadliest Ways Magic Can Go Wrong*, a book Mum didn't like the girls to read because it was full of unexpected and gruesome ways magical people had met unfortunate ends.

Being a successful sorcerer sometimes felt like mostly avoiding getting caught up in one of your own backfiring spells.

Raven had been slow to be convinced someone was making bad things happen at the school. But there was no getting away from the fact that someone wicked had put an end to lovely Mr Pickles in the soupy bottom of the school pond. It felt like a clear message and the chanting told her it wasn't only Morti who was starting to believe a witch was cursing Twinhills.

Grandpa Knox hadn't seemed to know the Howling Hag. That was strange. But why might she want to target the school? That was stranger. This other Twinhills witch was famous enough to have an inn named after her. But not famous enough to make an appearance in the book. Raven's reading turned into a fruitless search through many of the worst tales from the world of the Elysee sorcerers and she drifted into reading one her favourite tales. Nelly the Nervous had lived in a time when many people were superstitious and plenty believed in witches. So when crops started failing and cows' milk turned sour, the village elders got together and asked whether their village had been cursed. One visited a neighbouring seer, who suggested they might have upset Nelly, who lived deep in the surrounding forest, offering ancient cures to those who sought her out.

But instead of asking the seer for advice on how to soothe Nelly, the elder instead asked for directions on how to rid the village of her altogether.

The seer had looked into the future and said that killing a witch is not easy. You could hire a magical assassin, or find enough money to pay an even more powerful sorcerer to cast an unbreakable spell.

Instead of taking either of these options, the villagers hatched a plan to do it themselves on the cheap. They found a witch willing to offer a cut-price spell and they lured Nelly to a lonely place and used a half-baked curse that dissolved her into smoke. They drew the smoke into a stone cask and buried it and nothing was heard of Nelly for many years, long enough so that people believed everything told about her was just stories. But the seer had been right.

The villagers' plan had not killed Nelly. Instead, her spirit and the cask became one. When a small girl digging beneath a tree came across an interesting curved stone, she dug deeper. And that was how a small child named Lulu was taken over by Nelly's spirit and exacted a terrible revenge on the village.

Disappointingly, the tale was short on details of exactly how she exacted her revenge, although Raven and Rookery often speculated about it late into the night, and whether it was good that the witch won in the end, seeing as the villagers had behaved so badly and not even talked to Nelly nicely about whether she was even responsible for all the bad luck befalling them.

Dad refused to read it to them, not because it gave them nightmares (which it did; Raven was always sure their ideas about the revenge were even more imaginatively gruesome than what might have happened), but because it was a lot of old nonsense. Witches were not like that. That one was just a story, he soothed. But from reading several of Mum's suggested study texts, Raven knew it was all too real that sorcerers could choose to use their magic for evil, or to become powerful or rich.

A noise at the front door interrupted her reading. It was a welcome interruption because Raven felt she was going to have to face opening *A Most Utterly Comprehensive History of Magical Folk Ever*, almost too heavy to lift at over two thousand pages, if she was going to discover the hidden truth of the Howling Hag.

Morti Scratch was standing on the doorstep, a frown on his face in place of his usual smile. 'Did you not see?' He smoothed his over-long dark fringe out of his eyes.

'See what?'

'I was sending you a secret signal that it was safe for you to come over.'

Raven blinked at him.

'If you go to the attic room at the top of the inn and look out of the window, you can see right the way through to the bedroom at the top of your house. I was shining my torch right at you,' said Morti.

'I think the idea of a secret signal is not that you keep it a secret from the person you are signalling to,' said Raven helpfully. 'What is the signal anyway?'

'Three flashes with my torch. A pause. Then three more. Can I come in? We need to get moving if we're going to get on the trail of the Howling Hag, solve the murder of Mr Pickles, lift the curse and make school a bit more fun.'

'We're going to do all that? How exactly?'

'Luckily, I've been planning a battle strat to combat the malevolent forces of magic in Twinhills. Now she's gone and killed Mr Pickles there's no doubt the Howling Hag means business.' He had a foot over the doorstep when, from nowhere, that same black cat slipped past and got in ahead of him. 'Oo-er.' Morti took a startled step back. 'The Howling Hag's cat! It's following me,' he hissed. 'D'you think that means I'm going to be cursed next?'

The cat turned to look at him with her big green eyes.

'Or she might be hungry,' said Raven.

The cat padded about softly, sticking her pink nose into everything. It was the only part of her that wasn't glossily black. Morti was doing exactly the same, although without the pink nose. Raven tensed, ready to Deny Everything as Morti scoured the cluttered house with hungry, inquisitive eyes. What might she have missed this time?

'Er,' he began thoughtfully. 'I don't suppose you've got any biscuits, have you? Can't think when I'm hungry.'

After Bianca's visit and the exciting arrival of a full tin of chocolate biscuits, it was disappointing to discover how few were left. Especially when Morti helped himself to two. Raven watched him wolf them down, barely tasting them.

'So, you've got a strategy for how to track down who is behind these curses on the school?' said Raven.

'Yes, and to neutralize them.' Morti eyed the cat warily.

Raven had just been reading about how villagers had tackled Nelly by themselves and how badly that had turned out; she was not convinced that trying to neutralize a witch was necessarily the best course of action. Also, she couldn't ignore the fact that there was definitely one witch in Twinhills School. Neutralizing witches didn't sound great for her sister. Occasionally Rookery would risk a tiny bit of magic with people around, even though she shouldn't. Like when it was chocolate pudding day and the puddings always ran out too quickly. Yet no matter how late in the queue Rookery and Bianca were, Rookery would point to behind the ketchup or the water jugs and more chocolate treats were miraculously discovered.

No, Raven told herself. Chocolate pudding magic

was one thing. Rookery would never have neutralized Mr Pickles, or made those threatening words appear, or got Sam to have an accident so he burnt his hand. Morti was right. A malevolent magical force was at work. And she guessed they had to find out more before it caused any trouble for her very magical sister.

'What we need,' Morti crunched a third biscuit noisily, keeping a wary eye on the cat, 'is maybe a glass of milk? Perfect with these biscuits.'

The black cat let out a noisy miaow.

'I think the cat would like a glass of milk too. Actually, probably best make that a saucer.'

Raven passed Morti a glass and put down a saucer for the cat, who looked down, then up at her, miaowed and tiptoed to the door on soft paws.

'Not milk?' she asked the cat.

'Ooh, it's like she wants us to follow her,' said Morti, sounding excited.

The cat put her head on one side and blinked her big green eyes at them. 'Mrrrowwww.'

Morti lounged against one of the kitchen cupboards and dunked the remains of his biscuit in his glass of milk, watching the cat intently as she abandoned waiting by the door and went to lap up the milk. But then she quickly returned to the door.

Raven opened it, but the cat didn't go outside, just stood there miaowing really loudly.

'What do you think it wants?' asked Morti as Raven shut the door again.

The cat, exasperatingly, only pawed again at the closed door. Raven opened it again, but the cat hovered and refused to go outside, miaowing piteously now.

'Are you going out or staying in?' asked Morti. 'It really is like the cat wants us to follow it.'

'Mrrrowwww!' The cat began scratching at the door.

'Oh, this is ridiculous!' said a lilting female voice.

Raven found herself staring. Because those words had come from the cat.

'How much more obvious can I be?' said the lilting voice again, sounding even more exasperated. 'Of course I want you to follow me! I know I'm not supposed to do this, but can we just get over this whole *Oh, the cat talks* thing quickly. We've no time to hang about chatting if you want to find out who killed Mr Pickles. Come on!'

9. IT'S A TRICK

Morti's hands were twitching, his dark eyes shining.

'I think, I think . . . I know you'll find this difficult to believe, Raven, but, oh this is incredible . . . I think I have just discovered I am a sorcerer,' he hissed. 'I am probably a really powerful one, I can feel it.'

The cat blinked her big green eyes slowly.

'I can hear the cat's purring as *actual words*. I can understand what animals are saying!' Morti's face broke into a smile that took over his whole face. 'I

wonder what other magic I can do.' He took his glass of milk, put his hand over the top and closed his eyes. 'Maybe turn this milk into liquid gold.'

'No,' said the cat patiently. 'It's not you.' She extended a paw to Raven, who shook it. 'Nightshade, pleased to meet you.'

'There!' Morti pointed. 'When it lifted its paw. Ooh, d'you think the Howling Hag has cast a spell on me? At least it's a good one. Unless . . .' He looked at the black cat. 'You're not an evil demon, are you?'

'Actually, Morti, I heard the cat talk too,' said Raven.

There was a long silence, the sort that follows very unwelcome announcements: the cancelling of a day off school; birthday cakes with the wrong number of candles.

'The big news here is that you aren't magical.' Nightshade offered Morti a black paw to shake. 'But I am. Well, a bit.'

Morti stood perfectly still, his mouth open as if he was trying to drink in everything he was hearing in big greedy gulps. Then he punched the air. 'I knew it! Magic is real!'

Raven froze, picturing Mum's horror as she walked in and found her chatting about magic with Morti and a talking cat. *What was she doing?* Or

what had this cat done? Broken the Golden Rule –
in front of the nosy and inquisitive boy who
kept having to move because he was Trouble. Her
stomach went fluttery, a bit like it did when she
thought about her own magic never arriving. Some
things were so very difficult they just made you want
to hide in bed for a very long time with a duvet over
your head.

Morti's eyes gleamed almost as brightly as Nightshade's. 'You're Nightshade? Not Snoozy? But you're
the Howling Hag's cat?'

The hackles along Nightshade's spine raised.
'Whiskers and white mice. I'm nothing to do with
her. And I'm not, nor have ever been, Snoozy!'

'OK, that's good. Do you know you look like a
dimetrodon when your hackles do that,' said Morti.
'You know, the dinosaur with big spikes.' He said it
as if talking to cats was the most natural thing in the
world. 'Are you here to help us stop the Howling
Hag freaking out all the kids and stopping all our
fun?'

'Stopping your fun? I'm sure that is very important.' Nightshade began polishing her whiskers.
'What is possibly more serious is that soon everyone
at Twinhills is going to know magic is real. We need
to act fast. We need to track down who is cursing the

71

school and stop her or she's in danger of exposing the whole magical world.'

Morti was looking at Raven, then at Nightshade. 'Er, actually, plenty of the kids have told me if you put a toe out of line at Twinhills the local witch'll cut you up and eat you for breakfast. Never had that before and I've moved around *a lot*. I think you'll find half the kids at Twinhills already believe there's a witch. Think that cat's been out of the bag for some time.'

'Why was the cat in the bag to start with?' bristled Nightshade.

'It's just an expression,' soothed Raven, finding her voice at last.

She took a deep breath, the sort of breath you'd take if you were teetering on the edge of taking a plunge into very deep water.

'There are things I need you to get straight. Most importantly, Morti Scratch, there is a Golden Rule to never, ever reveal the secret of magic. Otherwise everyone would want all their problems solved with magic. This is a bigger deal than you can possibly know. It's enormous. And I have just broken it.' *What am I thinking even saying this to him?* But there seemed little point in Denying Everything. Not when faced with a talking cat. 'You have to keep this a secret, Morti.'

Morti's face creased in concentration as he chewed over everything. 'Yes. Of course. Cool. But magic's so exciting. We should tell everyone!'

'No!' cried Raven. 'That is not what I meant by keeping it a secret.'

'Raven's right,' said Nightshade, beginning to polish a paw. 'Imagine if completely the wrong person finds out that someone possesses extraordinary powers. What lengths might a bad person go to, to twist that magic and get control of it? You let everyone in on the secret about magic, suddenly everyone's looking about wanting a piece of the action. Magical folk'd be hounded into hiding.'

'If this Howling Hag is seriously not bothered about keeping the Golden Rule,' said Raven, 'that means trouble. And I don't just mean trouble with the Elysee – that's the organization that runs the magical world, Morti, and that would be bad – but trouble for all sorcerers.'

'Sorcerers?' Morti still sounded beyond excited. 'Right! Right.'

'The question you should be asking,' said Nightshade, beginning to wash her ears, 'is why someone is targeting a pleasant but unimportant school with magic. And how can we stop it. Because the murder of Mr Pickles means the Howling Hag is growing stronger. She's angry and she's nasty and we need to stop her.' She looked up at Raven. 'If you don't want Rookery to take the blame.'

'It really is curses and witchcraft, isn't it?' grinned Morti. 'I *love* Twinhills. We're going to get to the bottom of what's behind all the weird stuff, aren't we? We are going to be like detectives and investigate. Brilliant— Hang on a minute, your sister might take the blame? Why?'

'Because I bet strange things happen around Rookery all the time,' said Nightshade, blinking her green eyes. 'If we don't find out who's attacking the school with curses, your sister's days of living life as a normal witch will be over.'

'Normal witch! Heh heh!' Morti's eyes gleamed like moonlight reflected on still water as he looked at Raven. 'So, just to be clear, your sister is the main suspect because . . . she can do magic for real? Your Rookery's a witch?'

He looked completely excited, but Raven just felt as if she was swimming out of her depth and being swept away by the tide.

Strange things always did happen around Rookery. It was why Raven hadn't spotted quickly enough that someone else was doing magic.

Like the football match against their big rivals, Fivetors. One of the bigger Fivetors girls had been barging everyone out of the way, knocking over tiny Ella (most easily excited class chatterbox, most likely to say *isn't it sweeeet* about, well, almost everything). Ella had got to her feet, and then scored with a miraculous shot from the halfway line. Her first ever goal, and a virtually impossible one.

Ella was a hero, not least because it was the first time they had so much as drawn against Fivetors for years. And Rookery had been watching on the sidelines, her eyes turning from their catlike yellow to looking just a little bit smoky . . .

But these latest happenings were different. Rookery would never use her magic to do anything terrible. She wouldn't. OK, so there had been that little unfortunate incident with Henry Figgins and the pink paint . . . but there was no way Rookery was involved in the end of Mr Pickles. That was a clear message from the Howling Hag that her days of being sneaky were over and real trouble was about to begin.

'The general word is sorcerer,' explained Nightshade. 'Not everyone magical is a witch.'

'There's me,' chuckled Morti, 'going on about how it's all down to a witch, and you, Raven . . .'

Morti's eyebrows raised almost as far as his hair. 'You knew! How cool is that? So, are you like a family of witches? Does that mean you . . . ?'

'I might be,' answered Raven, her voice suddenly very small. 'But my affinity hasn't kicked in yet. Magic doesn't always run in families and my dad is not magical. My grandmother, Snapdragon, was the resident witch here in Twinhills for years, until . . . Now Grandpa Knox gets called on to do, you know, the odd spell, or charm. My mum is an Elysee curse breaker, so way too busy to do everyday witchcraft for people in Twinhills who still believe.'

'"The odd spell or charm"', Morti repeated, doing a fair cackle himself. 'We're ready for anything,' he said with relish. 'Sounds like you have a strat, Night-shade. I do have a question, actually, you know, before we head off to fight witches and stop their cackling . . . is it me, or does it seem ages since lunch?'

'Morti, now is not the time to think of food,' said Raven.

'Actually,' said Nightshade, scratching a hard-to-reach place in the centre of her back. 'I wouldn't say no to a nice piece of salmon. If you have one lying around. We've a hot walk ahead of us and no iced lemonade at the end of it.'

Raven made a general raid on the fridge, gathering things that covered everyone, and used the chance to gather her thoughts, darting another fearful glance at the door, thankful something was delaying Mum.

Nightshade sniffed like a restaurant critic at the dish Raven put before her. 'Oh yes, a nice piece of cheese will do very well. Is that cheddar? My favourite. Although a piece of fish is better. Just for the future, you know, if you wanted to get some in.'

The second she'd finished her snack she gave her whiskers a polish, stretched and padded for the door. 'To crack this case I'm going to need the help of you two humans. Finch is going to be back. We don't want to get entangled in a lot of infuriating questions. So let's go.'

'Where?' said Morti. 'What are we doing?'

'We go to the heart of the problem,' said Nightshade, plunging onwards, her tail in the air. 'We go where the children no longer dare. We go to Beechy Wood.'

PART TWO

10. WHAT THEY FOUND IN BEECHY WOOD

They followed Nightshade past the school and up to where a wooden sign pointed the way to the wood. Raven couldn't believe how soon they lost the heat of the day once they plunged under the cover of dark trees that grew protectively close. She couldn't help it; the second she could no longer see the sky, an involuntary shiver went down the full length of her spine.

Raven pushed on through the nettles and brambles snatching at her legs. The path was more

overgrown than she remembered and it felt as if the wood was punishing her for not visiting for so long. They passed the tree whose low branches concealed a den she and Rookery had made cosy over a number of years. Last summer, she and Rookery had spent as much time in Beechy Wood as possible. This summer Rookery hadn't even wanted to visit the swing Dad had set up for them.

Raven disentangled herself from a bramble that scratched viciously at her leg and reminded herself she had always loved this wood, with its unexpected dark hollows, shady corners and hidden rustlings.

'This is the place, isn't it?' Morti darted nervous looks everywhere. 'Where the Howling Hag lures children to cut 'em into pieces and eat 'em?'

'Not all witches live in woods and none lure in children to eat them,' replied Raven patiently. 'Those are just stories people like to tell to scare themselves.'

'You gotta remember, this witch stuff is not every-day for me.'

Nightshade was trotting ahead, oblivious to the thick undergrowth and the trees shutting out the sun and the clammy, dampening atmosphere, more shadow than cat.

Morti clutched at Raven's arm. 'Why do some

tree trunks look like faces? That one has, like, a big mouth just ready to open up and swallow you. And their branches are like long fingers reaching . . . Maybe it's the trees that come alive the minute your back's turned? Maybe it's the trees eating the kids alive, and not the witches.'

Raven moved with a determined bounce in her step, trying not to let Morti's fear spook her. Now was a good time to remember how Mum said that if you sound brave no one need know how you feel inside. 'Trees are just part of what's fun about woods.'

'There's a fun part?'

'That's the dragon tree, my favourite,' Raven pointed as they reached a dead tree where most of the branches had fallen, leaving a trunk shaped like a square-snouted dragon sniffing the air, and just a couple of branches that looked like short tyrannosaur-like arms. Crows cawed and circled above like sooty embers. 'Rookery and I always thought it looked like a dragon someone had defeated by turning it into a tree.'

'The Howling Hag turned a dragon into a tree?'

Raven sighed. 'No, we made it up.'

'What with the Howling Hag and the carnivorous trees, and the wild animals lurking and poisonous plants, giant spiders—' Morti turned sharply at an ominous creaking sound, like a monster sharpening its teeth. 'What was that?'

Raven pointed to where two branches were bending and rubbing together. 'It sounds a lot like a bird or an animal calling, but it's just branches creaking together. It's the trees talking.'

Morti stopped again, looking panicked as he disentangled himself from the clutches of grass and prickly brambles. Raven handed him a stout stick and pointed to a tiny blue butterfly fluttering past. 'There's a wild animal. Most of them are tiny and going to stay out of your way.'

Morti began fencing with the undergrowth, looking more confident once he was swiping like a sword-fighting pirate. 'I don't know woods – I've always lived in a city. With all the stories, I didn't dare come here on my own. It's so quiet. We could be the last people alive in the world.'

Raven grabbed his arm, making him jump, but she'd only wanted to stop him crashing about for a moment so she could point out a rabbit. 'If you stopped swishing and asking quite so many questions, you could hear a woodpecker. It's really not that quiet.'

Morti did stop. 'Yeah, you're right. I can hear a really ominous buzzing.' He edged nervously past a hawthorn blossom heavy with pollen, perfume and droning bees. 'So how do people know if they have magic? Could I be magical? I know a half-decent trick with a piece of string and a playing card. I can show you if you like.'

Raven was relieved when Nightshade took a turn answering Morti's relentless questions. She'd been beginning to think she'd need a spell to stop her ears falling off. Nightshade explained how there wasn't much call for a luck potion or a protective amulet once people stopped believing in curses. How people had stopped turning to witches for help. It was why magic was now incredibly rare and why sorcerers stayed secret.

'There's not enough magic to go around if every-one wanted some. Yet there was a time when you could trip over a magical person in pretty much every village. Also, magic is hard work. It can take years of practice to do magic well and sorcerers stopped thinking it was worth the bother of doing the training. And as magic doesn't always get passed on in families, gradually the old ways, the old teachings, all started to fade. Magic is dying out.'

'Dying out!' Morti stopped his swooshing. 'That's rotten bad luck. The dying-out part is bad, specially as I only just found out it was real. Guess the chances of me being magical aren't huge?'

They were in the darkest part of Beechy Wood now, where the trees were so thick you could not even see the fence that separated the wood from the school. Raven shivered again. You wouldn't know it was a bright and sunny day.

'Are we nearly there?' Morti asked.

'Not far to what I want to show you,' answered Nightshade, taking a right-hand fork that Raven knew swung around the back of the school. 'You'll recognize it in a bit. There's a gate you go through with Miss Percy for your survival lessons.'

'You know so much about our school. Have you been keeping us under surveillance?' Morti said. 'Are you a police cat?'

'You think the police have cats? You get police dogs, but that always seems one big mistake. A police cat would be so much better. Cats go about things without making half so much fuss and noise as dogs.'

'I knew it! A detecto-cat. And you've been drawn here to Twinhills by your special magical cat senses that detect bad sorcerers at work.'

'Not entirely,' answered Nightshade, her tail swinging behind her. 'I'm mostly here for a holiday.'

'Ha! Undercover. You can't fool us. I bet you solve magical crimes all over the place.'

'I may have been responsible for clearing up a few high profile and very tricky cases. Did you know in Ancient Egypt, cats were worshipped?' Nightshade dodged as Morti swooshed his stick left and right. 'The best Twinhills has to offer is a decent piece of salmon once a day at the Maudlins'. At least there is one family who know how to treat a cat.'

'Well, me and Raven only just decided there was anything to investigate. We never expected a cat to be a few steps ahead of us.'

'That,' said Nightshade, 'is because humans do tend to underestimate cats. Which can be a little annoying. And humans do tend to take the credit.'

'Ooh well, we are happy to be your sidekicks, aren't we, Raven? If you are going to teach us detectiving skills we need a name.'

'I don't think so.'

'Not for our gang or anything.'

'Good.'

'I mean like a case file name. Operation Nighthawk.'

'Nighthawk?'

'Dunno. Better than Operation Get the Witch— Oh, sorry Raven, I didn't mean your sister.'

The path had become almost completely over-grown. Raven thought there was no way through, even with Morti's stick. But almost magically, the trees parted, revealing baked ground beginning to crack after weeks without rain. Snaking tendrils squished underfoot and added to the wood sap and resiny smell of the forest. They had reached a clearing, an almost circular patch of welcome sunshine.

'I know where we are!' cried Morti. 'We've walked right around to the back gate of the school. Right by the biggest tree in Beechy Wood. The hanging tree,' he said with relish, and put his head back to look up at a mighty oak. It had branches that reached far into the sky and some that dipped low towards the school. 'Bet there's a terrible tale about this tree?'

Raven's thoughts were going down an uncomfortable little path of their own. When Miss Percy unlocked the back gate and brought them through to their forest lesson, Raven always walked as quickly as possible past the hanging tree. It had a very bad connection with her family.

Nightshade carried on into the clearing with her quick, shadowy movements. Finally she paused by the remains of a fire, dipping her pink nose towards it. 'This is what I wanted to show you.'

'Yeah, that'll be Miss Percy's fire,' said Morti, sounding disappointed. 'She does these fantastic whole-school lessons in things like how to find dry wood to start a fire even if it's been raining. She took us right up the top of Uphill once and we made rope out of nettles. Pretty much everyone stung their hands. But it was good fun.'

'But Miss Percy always does small, neat fires,' Raven pointed out, looking at the fire. 'She'd never let her fires get as big as this.'

'Yeah, but this fire could've been here ages,' Morti said, poking at the soft grey ash with his toe.

'That pile of ash has got bigger since last week,' explained Nightshade. 'Yesterday, bits were still warm. And Miss Percy didn't bring you all this week.'

'You're right!' breathed Morti, flinging himself full length on to the grass. 'So how could it be warm? So someone's been secretly in these woods just at the back of the school.'

'That seems very probable,' said Nightshade.

'Our first piece of evidence and our first lesson in being honorary detecto-cats! We are on the Howling Hag's trail. So she's living in this wood and using fire to do her magic? Or is that stuff about brewing things up in cauldrons just stories? Like the broomsticks and cackling thing?'

Raven answered. 'No, cauldrons are pretty accurate.'

'You rest your paws now, Raven.' Nightshade settled down alongside Morti, tucking her own four paws underneath her. 'Because I have important things to tell. So far the Howling Hag is having everything her own way. It's not going to be easy to stop her.'

Raven flopped next to them wearily in the heat.

'The murder of Mr Pickles,' said Morti. 'That was like the perfect crime. No witnesses.'

'Morti, you are absolutely right,' said Nightshade.

Morti beamed.

'The very fact no one saw anything means it's not a good place to start. We need to begin with a curse that gives us people we can talk to.'

'Interrogate,' breathed Morti.

'If we assume that whoever is doing the curses killed Mr Pickles, then we start where the Howling Hag has made one mistake. I want to tell you what I know of the Curse of the Impossible Theft.'

'Is an impossible theft a curse, just to be clear . . . ?' Morti tailed off as Nightshade glowered at him with her big green eyes.

'OK. Let's call it the Curse of the Vanishing Money.'

11. A Thief in the School

Above Miss Percy's classroom there's a nice patch next to the skylight in the wooden roof that's always been warmed by the sun if I arrive just after first break. It's my second favourite spot after a branch in that hanging tree. I was listening to Miss Percy's class planning their Aztec masks, having fun daring each other to make them as grotesque and terrifying as possible. The smell of paint and glue drifted up along with cheerful voices.

I may even have dozed into a light snooze, because

the next thing I knew was a chorus of high voices discussing whether the roast potatoes would have run out before they got to the front of the lunch queue.

I expected Miss Percy to take out the chicken salad sandwich she always ate for lunch and head to the staffroom. But instead, towering Miss Percy, Twinhills' warrior queen – put her head in her hands and groaned.

This woke me right up, but there was no way to slip off my roof and go and offer a little comfort. Anyway, I wasn't the only one who noticed. Miss Sunny bustled in right away from the next-door classroom where she had been teaching about mosaics. She demanded to know what was wrong and Miss Percy's mouth tightened in disappointment.

'I'm afraid to say we have a thief in the class.'

Miss Percy opened her special drawer and unlocked the box where things were placed for safe keeping until they could be handed back at the end of the day. The box was empty. Miss Sunny looked shocked.

'I've always felt I know the children so well. But I've failed. There's one I don't know at all. And I don't even understand how it could have happened,' Miss Percy said helplessly.

Miss Sunny perched on the edge of one of the small desks and asked Miss Percy to tell her everything. I was just as eager to hear.

Two days before, Sian had handed in a twenty-pound note, proudly saying in front of the class she was off to watch a film with her cousin and the money meant they were to have plenty of sweets and popcorn. Unfortunately, Sian went down with a chill and a bad cough that day and was sent home. The twenty-pound note had sat in Miss Percy's desk since then and had been joined that morning by a very interesting piece of granite that Ella had found on her way into school and wanted kept safe in Miss Percy's special drawer.

'What is really strange is that stone has vanished too,' said Miss Percy, looking even more puzzled. 'Not just the twenty pounds.'

'Oh no, poor Ella!' Miss Sunny's face creased in concern. 'The stone wasn't valuable?'

'I can't imagine it was. It was pretty – a glittery green with a couple of lines of white quartz, and a hole through it. Some people do think those stones are lucky. But I locked that stone away before morning lessons so I know the money was there. Something made me check just now. The box was empty, but I just don't understand . . .' Miss Percy looked about her, then at the ceiling, as if hoping the answer would appear.

'That's terrible,' murmured Miss Sunny. 'Maybe it's . . . maybe it's a prank. There have been a few strange things happening at the school. Perhaps it'll turn up, like Ella's shoes suddenly reappearing on the spelling trophy. Maybe someone thinks these things are funny, although poor Ella was so upset.'

Miss Percy didn't return Miss Sunny's reassuring smile.

'You said you saw the money first thing and it was gone by lunch – well then,' said Miss Sunny, 'you can probably work it out. Who would have had the chance to take it?'

Miss Percy looked thoughtful for a moment and I listened in closely.

There was plenty of chatter about strange happenings plaguing the school. It sounded as if this might be a chance to find out who was sneaking into classrooms, making unsettling things happen and stuff vanish without anyone seeing anything. Could Miss Percy narrow down the suspects and give a clue to who was behind it? I found myself holding my breath.

But she only sighed. 'The whole thing is so strange. I don't know how anyone managed it at all because the box was still locked.' She frowned at the small box. 'In fact, the more I think about it, the stranger it gets.'

Miss Percy explained how the key was kept safe in a zipped pocket in her bag under the desk. 'My wallet is in that bag. If someone wanted to steal money, why dig around and unzip that pocket for the keys to the box, go the drawer and unlock it? They could simply have taken some cash from my wallet. And the key is exactly where I left it. It's like some vanishing trick.'

'It's not like you to say things like that!' said Miss Sunny, her face breaking into a smile. 'I guess it's up to me to be practical. Come on. When could it have been taken? We'll solve your locked-box mystery!'

I had been listening carefully, but I really pricked up my ears when Miss Percy called the whole thing a trick. Because it was a puzzle – if someone had simply wanted to steal money, they could have simply pinched her wallet. Why had they gone to the bother of opening the box? Perhaps it wasn't about the money. These incidents at the school really did seem to be mostly about unsettling people. And Miss Percy was clearly worried.

Miss Sunny went on briskly, 'Well, we can rule out it being stolen during lessons, if someone had to rummage in your bag. That must narrow it right down.'

Miss Percy considered carefully. 'It could only have happened in first break. I had to take a call in the office, so the classroom was empty.'

Miss Sunny's usually cheerful smile compressed itself into a firm line. 'Yours was, but not mine. I was at my desk throughout the whole of break time and I can see right into your classroom. The thief may not have realized that.'

'Someone came into my classroom?' said Miss Percy slowly.

It sounded like Miss Sunny had seen something. Was it possible that between them, these two teachers were going to give a clue to who was really behind all these curses?

Miss Sunny winced. 'Several people. Aaliyah came straight back in, of course, to tidy away the pencils and glue sticks as usual.'

'Such a helpful, thoughtful child,' said Miss Percy. 'She doesn't like being noisy and boisterous with the others outside at break, that's the reason she's always in at break time. Anyone else?'

Miss Sunny nodded. 'Carsen Samuels came in because he'd lost a plaster on his finger. I spoke to him and sent him to Mrs Maudlin and the first aid box in the office. So he knew he'd been seen. But two of your girls came in. I heard them talking about looking for a sunhat, thought it might be on a peg in the cloakroom.' It was Miss Sunny's turn to look thoughtful as she recreated a scene in her mind. 'I don't think they knew I was there.'

'Who?'

(I knew things about my story were not going to go down well with Raven, but there was no way to avoid mentioning the two girls Miss Sunny named: Bianca Maudlin and Rookery Charming. I pressed hurriedly on to the point where Miss Percy asked if there was anyone else.)

'Well, yes . . . there was one other person. I mean, if you are going to be thorough.' Miss Sunny tapped her fingers on her chin. Miss Sunny had gone on talking mostly to herself, slipping deeper in thought. 'He might not have known I saw him. I didn't speak to him. I guess, to be fair, we have to count him.'

'Who?' prompted Miss Percy, sounding impatient. 'Who was it?'

'Well, I hate to mention it, but it was Mr Odorless.'

12. OUR NUMBER ONE SUSPECT

'Mr Odorless?!' Morti and Raven chorused together. My whiskers twitched, but I'd suspected they might react like this.

'Hang on a minute! No way!' Morti propped himself up on his elbows to stare and splutter: 'You gotta be kidding me. So, just to be clear, we've got to investigate Mr Odorless?'

I might as well have told them they were going into a lion's den with only one of Knox's jam tarts to defend them.

'I thought you were ready to head off on your rusty steeds to fight witches and nothing was going to stop you.' I turned over a paw and extended my claws.

'Yeah, but when you said we could be detectives and investigate, I never thought you meant Mr Odorless!' complained Morti. 'This is bad.' Morti's smile had run away completely. 'I didn't even know head teachers could be witches, but now you've said it, have you noticed he is always there, you know, like magic, if ever I do something I'm not supposed to?'

I began to wash my ears. 'That might not require magic. That might just happen because you are quite often doing something you're not supposed to.'

Morti's face creased in concentration as he chewed over everything.

I padded to the edges of the clearing to stretch and scratch on the trunk of the lovely gnarly old hanging tree. Morti followed me, firing questions.

'So you are saying Mr Odorless, Aaliyah, Carsen, Rookery, Bianca and for fairness I guess Miss Percy and Miss Sunny . . . No. I'm not sure exactly what you're saying . . . The Howling Hag . . . nope. I'm gonna need a much bigger download about magic.'

'Magic is complicated,' I explained patiently. 'But to steal that stone and the money from a locked box in a drawer, someone would have to get near, even using magic.'

'We need to find out if any of them saw anything,' Raven suggested.

'Saw the Howling Hag, you mean?' said Morti. 'But wouldn't you say if you spotted some old witch creeping into the school from these woods?'

Raven pointed out that Morti should have understood by now that witches don't actually look like the picture outside the inn.

'I know, I know, witches basically just look like your sister.'

'It certainly isn't Rookery!'

Morti began to prod the undergrowth with his stick, as if hoping to discover a witch hiding in the bracken. I wondered exactly what he thought he'd find – a tiny wooden door to her house? What would he do if he found her?

'Why would anyone steal from a locked box when they could easily have taken money from Miss Percy's wallet. Nope – magical crime makes no sense.'

'I think you will find,' I said, 'that the fact none of it makes sense is kind of what makes it a mystery. That's why we have to investigate.'

But it was a good question and one I kept asking myself.

Raven had stayed by the grey remains of the fire, her face solemn. I watched her retrieve something from the ashes that she sneaked into her pocket, saying nothing.

Morti prodded wildly at a big hole in a tree and a bird shot out with a shrill cry and a flutter of terrified wings. Morti's shriek was even louder and he jumped so far in the air it looked like he was trying to take off. That stopped him poking at everything and he flopped back on the warm grass, unusually silent and his happy face troubled.

If he was thinking that investigating a magical crime sounded so difficult that it might not be worth starting, I wouldn't blame him. We were up against it.

'I was just wondering . . . I don't suppose you brought a few of those nice biscuits with you, Raven?' he said. 'Could really do with a little snackage right now.' He rummaged in his pockets and produced a very flat-looking packet of crisps. 'Otherwise it's prawn cocktail. Anyone?' Morti rolled on to his back and pointed upwards. 'Everly's kite got stuck up there. Her uncle bought her this fantastic kite and they went right out to try it. And some freak gust of wind made the kite get tangled. Bet that was the Howling Hag's bad magic!'

'Gusts of wind do tend to do that with kites,' I said.

'Everly was in tears. Next day, the kite was just sitting on her desk in the classroom when she came into school! Everyone was gobsmacked. Weird stuff happens all the time at this school.'

'Actually,' said Raven in a small voice. 'Rescuing the kite was probably Rookery – it's the sort of thing she could do with her powers and she has the thoughtfulness and the patience to do it.'

'Well, that's going to complicate things if some of this magic is down to Rookery,' complained Morti. 'How will we tell her magic from the Hag's? OK – go. You are the magical experts – how do we even investigate a magical crime?'

'It's not so different from any other crime. We establish facts, look for motives, narrow the suspects,' I said, settling down in the sunshine. 'We pay attention to detail.' They hadn't quite yet seen the whole picture. I'd have to get to that.

'Follow clues?' suggested Morti.

'Exactly. Your first lesson in being a good detective is that you need to get people to tell you things. Then be perceptive. That means sort the truth from the lies. You will find, when you have been detecting as long and successfully as I have, that almost everyone has secrets – something inside of them they feel guilty about and they would much rather other people don't know. Then you have to work out which secrets are important.'

Raven continued sitting silently. She had completely lost her bounce. It was unfortunate I'd had to include her sister in the list of people we needed to talk to, but we had to start somewhere.

Morti muttered, '*Facts, motives, details, suspects, lies*. Cool!'

'Morti,' Raven began, 'someone told you there was a *legend* of the Howling Hag – nonsense about luring children into the wood to eat them. A legend sounds like a witch who lived years ago. But the curses are happening right now. Plus Grandpa Knox had never heard of the Howling Hag. Is that the sort of little detail you mean?' She turned to me hopefully.

'Knox might have got in a muddle?' I suggested.

Morti looked upwards. 'Thought you were going to tell me the hanging tree has got something to do with the legend?' He pointed upwards and dropped his voice to a hushed whisper. 'Here's an idea. Maybe the villagers in olden times got rid of unwanted people by . . . you know?' He drew his finger theatrically across his throat.

'That's my favourite tree for watching the school, if you don't mind,' I said, but that didn't stop him.

'P'raps the Howling Hag was killed here. Now she's back and living in the wood and exacting her revenge.'

'Morti,' Raven said. 'Even magical people can't bring back the dead.'

'Well, technically there is a branch of sorcery that's devoted to—' I stopped at a sharp look from Raven.

'And ghosts are not likely to light fires,' Raven added quickly, keen to squish down his more fanciful ideas about magic. We had our work cut out there too.

Then she surprised me by saying: 'Although, I was looking up the Howling Hag earlier and there is a story that sounds similar to what Morti just said – villagers tried to kill a witch called Nelly, but only killed her body, not her spirit. She came back for revenge. But Dad said all that was nonsense.'

'Woah! We really are dealing with a vengeful spirit magical ghost,' said Morti. He sounded pleased, thrilled and scared all at the same time – more the reaction I'd have expected if someone had told him he was being taken skydiving for his birthday. 'So, basically, what is our strat for solving Operation Pickles?'

'Operation Pickles?' I queried.

'Someone had to decide on a name. We need to plunge headlong into Operation Pickles Alpha Phase. Before we think about how terrifying it all is.'

Raven leapt to her feet. 'Just being here is creeping me out. Can we go?'

We started to wind our way back, Morti unstoppably full of ideas and questions.

'Ooh,' he said, his eyes gleaming. 'How about this. Is the stone that was stolen magical? Ella showed it me and it was weird and glittery.'

'Someone just happened to find a magical stone lying around?' I said.

'Don't see why not, especially here in Twinhills where all these witches secretly hang about. Although Ella got proper upset, you know, after that trick with her shoes, and then her stone. Bianca was kind and found her another even shinier stone the next day and then Ella wasn't so bothered. So I guess probably not magical.'

Raven shrugged. 'If we had the stone we could have looked into whether there was anything magical about it that would make it worth stealing.'

Morti wanted to know how.

'It's my mum's skill – detecting magic,' Raven said. 'Using magic leaves ripples in the air. She uses this special bracelet to see them and work out what magic's been used. That enables her to break curses. But we don't have the stone.'

'Morti could be right,' I said. 'The theft might not have been about the money at all. If we could find where that stone is . . . '

Morti looked pleased for a second, then groaned again. In fact, he moaned the whole walk back. 'She'd have to get near that box. I get that. I still say this Howling Hag could be hiding in the woods, she could be taking some sort of revenge. But how is she getting into school without anyone noticing? Even if she looks like anyone. Invisibility? You're going to tell me that's not real either. Operation Pickles. We're only on Alpha Phase and already it's impossible.'

'It's a good point and actually, I do have a little theory.' I snaked my tail. 'One I should probably mention.' I didn't think this is what they mean by saving the best until last, but they needed to know.

'As long as it's some good news. Preferably something that gets us out of interrogating old Odorless,' said Morti. 'I haven't forgotten that part.'

'It's more of a warning,' I said. 'One explanation for all these curses is that it is slightly possible that . . . someone has inherited the Howling Hag's magic.'

'Inherited?' Raven looked as terrified as if Mr Odorless had appeared.

'How does that work?' asked Morti as we reached the high street and burst back out into dazzling sunshine.

'Someone in Twinhills, someone at your school, could be a descendant of the Howling Hag,' I said quietly.

'Hang on a minute,' said Morti. 'That's why you keep saying that witches can look like anyone. That's why no one is seen sneaking into the school. I get it! That's what you mean by narrowing down our suspects? We shouldn't just talk to Mr Odorless, Aaliyah, Carsen, Rookery, Bianca, Miss Percy or Miss Sunny to find out if they saw anything as they were the ones at the scene of the crime – you're saying one of them actually *is* the Howling Hag?'

13. OPERATION PICKLES – ALPHA PHASE

Raven had tried so many kinds of magic. She'd tried to blow out candles with her mind. She'd tried to lock doors with a charm where all you had to do was learn to say the right words – *drusyn caw-giflyn*. It felt about as magical as chewing a tough bit of meat. And about as successful. The locks didn't so much as squeak.

Mum never lost patience, but simply passed over more spells that were scratched on well-worn scrolls of parchment curling at the edges. Spells based on so

many different magical affinities it made Raven's head swim. Mum said they were all simple enough to have kick-started the magic of hundreds of sorcerers throughout the ages. Just not Raven's.

Another day, yet another type of magic. And Raven could do none of it.

Yesterday, just before they'd let Nightshade head off for her daily salmon feast at the Maudlins', Morti had made them come up with a strategy for Operation Pickles. They'd agreed to each take one of the suspects. Nightshade and Morti had argued, but finally agreed they would take on fearsome Mr Odorless together. They'd sneak in and search his house for clues, only because this was slightly less terrifying than having to interrogate him. Raven had been cowardly, shrinking at even the idea of breaking into Tidy House.

If she was serious about trying to expose any new witch determined to stir up magical trouble in Twinhills, she should have been the one to do the breaking in. Yet she had left that job to Morti Scratch and the talking cat.

Well, she would just have to make a really good job of another part of Alpha Phase – to comb all the magical books she could for all available intel to help them defeat the Howling Hag – or her descendant.

Oh. And investigate her own sister.

Mum would be out most of today and Raven said she'd head to Knox's. Instead, once she heard Rookery and Bianca chattering in the lane that wove up to Bianca's, Rookery getting updates on the latest hamster news, Raven secretly slipped back into a silent and empty house. This was her chance.

She twirled the shiny finial on the side of the fireplace that made the bookcase revolve and revealed the room where Mum kept the tools of her trade – including a generous selection of magical books. She was determined to track down the Howling Hag's connection with Twinhills and find out what had happened to her.

Asking Mum would only lead to awkward questions Raven couldn't possibly answer, not without it all spilling out just how many secrets Raven was keeping. There was the horrible fact that Raven had utterly blown Denying Everything. This made Raven go hot and then cold. Then there was her constant fear that Rookery's magic was somehow involved in what was happening at school. This was before she even started on the terrible thought that she was close to admitting she had no magic. She could not even imagine a future without it.

She heaved *A Most Utterly Comprehensive History*

of Magical Folk Ever off the shelf and started turning its two thousand pages.

Mostly she read these books hoping for a spark, some flicker of recognition of what magic she might be able to do. She knew about charms and curses; Mum specialized in those. She had learnt about magical science – disguising magic within everyday objects (like a specolens that Snapdragon had built to keep an eye on who might be coming to call at Dandelion Cottage). Really powerful magical artefacts were the sort of treasured objects that only the very wealthy could afford and only very skilled magical scientists could create.

More and more she was drawn to read about the magical frauds. Like Professor Perfidious. He had sold thousands of bottles of his truth potion before someone tricked him into drinking his own spell and asked him how it worked. He could pretend it had worked, he *had* been charmed, and he was compelled to tell the truth . . . but whatever potion recipe he gave wouldn't work when someone else made it, revealing he was a fraud. Or he could refuse to tell, but that was only going to reveal that his own potion didn't work and he didn't have a clue how to do any magic . . . and he would be revealed as a fraud anyway.

Whichever he chose was going mark the end of a lucrative business.

Within the space of twenty-four hours, Professor Perfidious went from being a rich and successful man to a confused and broken one and he was offered a room at the Retreat for the Magically Impaired and Disappointed. Raven had begun to feel she was going to end up there if her magic didn't kick in soon.

She turned more pages. What was the Howling Hag's story? Could she have a descendant living among them in Twinhills? Raven turned pages more feverishly. But the Howling Hag had been either too daft or too devious to make it into the books of notable witches and wizards. Her only place in history appeared to be that she'd had an inn named after her. This was going to be another thing Raven was going to fail at.

Pretty much everything made Raven feel that she had a rip of wrong inside of her. The only way to deal with it had been to give that hollow place a name. The Not Good Enough hole. Neg, she'd started calling it, because she wasn't even good at acronyms.

Neg niggled inside her right now, telling her the Howling Hag was notorious enough to have an inn named after her, so she should be able to find her.

Why couldn't she? Because she was useless at everything, that was why.

She closed the heavy book with a snap. She
pressed the finial to slide back the revolving bookcase and hide the secret room, hating to admit she'd
failed. But she had another task she needed to do
while the house was empty.

She had promised to investigate her sister and she
could not miss her chance and fail at that too.

The Howling Hag had stolen Ella's sparkly green
stone and the twenty pounds from a locked box. All
Raven had to do to prove Rookery's innocence
was tell the others she did not have the stone, or
the money. Or anything that might link her to the
terrible death of Mr Pickles. Or anything that might
prove she had come up with any sort of spell to make
Sam Carruthers burn his hand, or make the warning
I am here and I am going to eat you appear on Miss
Sunny's board.

Raven reached into her pocket and touched what
she had rescued from the fire. She would think
about that later.

Even though she was alone in the house, Raven
paused at the top of the stairs to listen for a moment
before sneaking into her sister's neat room.

She knew the sort of places Rookery would hide

something. She started with the chest of drawers, moved quickly to the bedside table and under the mattress and behind a shelf of her sister's books.

Rookery possessed such a very useful sort of magic. She could move things just by focusing and thinking hard. It was magic that didn't need a secret room, years of learning, or lots of standing around cauldrons.

Rookery was destined to become famous for her incredible magic. Raven would get a job like Dad, one where you had to know your times tables and the capitals of ever so many countries.

But Rookery could not be responsible for the curse on the school.

Yet as Raven tackled the wardrobe, it was bothering her that Rookery no longer talked about what troubled her. When she and Raven used to talk about everything, Rookery had explained that things often happened without her even meaning them. Like that boy who'd been bullying a small kid when they'd been at Fivetors. He'd fallen flat on his face in the mud and everyone had laughed. Was that cruel or kind?

Raven delved further, unable to stop herself thinking of that little trouble with Henry Figgins. Rookery had been putting the finishing touches to one of her best-ever paintings when Henry had spilled dirty water for cleaning brushes all over it. Accidents do happen, he'd said.

Henry was best in the school at science, as well as being the much-envied holder of the 'Knobbliest Knees' trophy (awarded annually at the Fivetors and Twinhills Annual Horticultural Carnival). Yet he was most proud of his arty picture of a starlit sky, entitled *Night Sky*. It had been awarded first prize at the Twinhills School Photography Club Competition.

Rookery had screwed up her ruined picture and told Henry she didn't mind. But then, suddenly, Henry somehow squirted himself with pink paint. It was just before he was about to accept his Best Photograph rosette and certificate in assembly. Well, accidents do happen.

Raven finally found what she was hunting for: Rookery's box of treasures hidden in a shoe box right in the bottom of her wardrobe, under an untidy pile of colourful jumpers it was far too hot to wear at the moment. Raven took out the box. Rookery had used it to collect things on their adventures in Beechy Wood; a shimmering tail feather, a once-shiny conker.

She hoped against all hope that she would not lift the lid and see that stone, or the twenty pounds. Or any other signs that her sister had got herself involved in something bad.

She had just lifted the lid when the sound of the front door opening made her jump. But not as much as what she saw in Rookery's treasures box.

She hadn't even time to be scared. She replaced the box hurriedly and jumbled some jumpers over it, and ran downstairs where Mum was standing by a book Raven had left out, one Mum would approve of her reading.

'Oh, well done, Raven, you've made a start without me. Sorry I'm late.'

But not as sorry as Raven was.

The second she'd lifted that lid she'd found herself staring at something horrible. Not the stone, not the money, but a mask – a nasty thing, a blank face, with slits for eyes. But more than that. It had a hood that would go right over your head and would completely cover up who you were. You really would not want to come across anyone wearing a mask like that.

What could Rookery possibly be doing with it? Was this magic? If so, it was magic Raven knew nothing of at all.

Now she had yet another secret to keep.

Now she really had no idea what to do.

14. ALL ABOUT DOGS (UNFORTUNATELY)

Morti should have been here by now. I stretched out along the sun-dappled wall and checked my claws. Where was he? Had he abandoned me to tackle the beast on my own?

We'd had a bit of an argument. That small snappy creature who thought yapping was clever was not something I wanted to run into when I was searching Mr Odorless's house. Morti and Raven were more worried about old Odorless himself.

Raven had made the very reasonable observation

that if Odorless was the Howling Hag's descendant and was cursing the school, he'd have magical things about and all we had to do was nip into Tidy House and take a quick peek around.

'Nip into his house?' echoed Morti.

It was a great idea. 'Well, don't look at me,' I'd protested. 'He's got a great big dog.'

'He's got some tiny, yappy terrier thing that's about the size of a rat,' scoffed Morti.

'And how scary do you think a dog's teeth are when you're my size?'

'OK, point taken. But er, hang on, Raven – are you seriously suggesting we break into Mr Odorless's house and search for a cauldron or something?' Morti had said.

'Probably not a cauldron,' mused Raven. 'He's more likely to have magical books. And if he's got Ella's stone we'll prove he stole it.'

'So we sneak into his house and search it for a tiny stone?' Morti had said. 'Right, that makes a lot of sense. Can see that's going to be a big help.'

'No, of course we don't have to do that at all,' I'd said. 'Not if you've got a better suggestion.'

'You just need a simple plan to make sure Mr Odorless and Titus are out,' said Raven.

'All right,' Morti had groaned. 'You and me,

Nightshade, we'll be spies. I'll be the distraction and lookout. *You* go covert and break into his house. You'll need to be a stealth cat.'

I'd pinged my claws. 'I think you'll find I am always a stealth cat.'

Now I twitched my tail impatiently. This was so not how taking on two human sidekicks was supposed to work out. I was meant to send *them* to do the sneaking around and the dangerous stuff while I sat and pondered all the fiendish clues between naps.

Morti only lived at the inn next door – what on earth was taking him so long? Because Carsen Samuels was now wandering along, whistling tunelessly, hands in pockets, heading for Mr Odorless's house. I had little choice but to act.

I slunk off the wall and did the usual. Rubbed around his legs. Carsen was a friendly boy, a nice soft shape like a ripe pear, perhaps not the obvious choice to ask to exercise your dog. Raven had told me he was best in the school at jokes. And the one who never forgot to take marshmallows to share on Miss Percy's regular fire-lighting and bushcraft sessions. Raven was very good at spotting people's talents.

I delayed Carsen as long as I could and finally the rickety gate to the inn flung open and Morti tore through, hurtled towards Carsen and skidded to a halt.

'Hi! You're off to walk the pooch, aren't you?' Morti said breathlessly. 'I thought I'd come with you.'

What had happened to the carefully constructed plan? Morti was supposed to stroll past at just the moment to make it look as if he was just happening to stop, just to be friendly. I'd told him Carsen was bound to be fed up walking that piece of carpet every day as he only did it because Mr Odorless paid him. Morti was to keep him busy as long as possible.

Not surprisingly, Carsen looked suspicious at this sudden enthusiasm bursting at him from nowhere. I relied on Morti to say the right thing.

'I thought about an hour, you know. It's a good length of walk for a dog,' said Morti. 'Shall we go?'

I would have put my head in my paws. This lack of basic detecting skills was making my whiskers ache.

Carsen shrugged and clicked open the gate, and they walked along the straight path lined with white stones that Mr Odorless bleached regularly. The boys were careful not to step on the immaculate square lawn, edged with weed-free borders and waxy geraniums a regulation fifteen centimetres apart.

Carsen let himself in the back door with a key and a low white rug hurled itself out in a frenzy of barking.

This was the trickiest bit. This was the bit we had gone over and over in the plan.

'Where d'you take him?' asked Morti, sliding sideways to move between Carsen and the back door. 'How about Beechy Wood?' He moved to point and shuffled to block Carsen's view of the inside of the house. 'Guess you could throw sticks and stuff in there.'

Carsen turned to look towards the wood behind him and shuddered. 'I'm not going up there.' He bent to click on Titus's lead.

'Nah. It's all scuttling and insects, isn't it? Even the trees make ominous noises, like they're coming to life. So where are we going?'

Carsen closed the door and locked it. Titus strained and the barking reached fever-pitch. He hurled himself against the door as if the last thing he wanted was to go on a walk. I guessed Titus hadn't missed what happened. Because the boy had done good. Morti had given me just enough of a moment to play my stealth cat part. I'd slipped inside.

'Want me to hold that lead? You've hurt your hand. How'd you do that? Did you burn it the same as Sam?' asked Morti as they began to walk.

Carsen jerked Titus's lead a little unkindly as the pooch was having a good sniff at the bottom of a passing cat.

'None of your business.'

Titus made a dash, yanking his lead and dragging Carsen in the direction of the sign that pointed to Beechy Wood. The lead almost jerked out of Carsen's hand. I was watching from the window, but even I could see he was having difficulty because of the plasters wrapped around two of his fingers.

'No, you're probably right.' Morti slipped along after him. 'You might think I'm a bit annoying to start with, but you'll find out that I'm all right when you get to know me. My parents run pubs and we move around all the time so I'm pretty good at making friends. Why do lots of Miss Percy's class have plasters on their fingers? Makes me wonder what you are all doing.'

Carsen was Morti's target suspect and I left him to his own interrogation techniques. Mr Odorless was mine. Walking Titus was what they call killing two birds with one stone.

I saw Morti turn and look back, his face one big grin. For a moment I thought he was going to give us away by giving me a big thumbs up, but he, Carsen and Titus just carried on walking. Titus stopped at a patch of soft earth and began digging in with his paws, spraying dirt in all directions before cocking his leg. Honestly, why anyone ever prefers dogs to cats is a mystery.

I silently wished Morti luck, but I had work to do. I had to trust that he could keep Carsen and the annoying rug out of the way for long enough to let me do my bit in peace.

15. The Curse of an Evil Witch

'Well, I'm not abandoning Odorless as a suspect totally.' Morti was stretched full length on the grass. Nightshade lounged next to him like a puddle of darkness, her tail giving a tiny twitch every now and again.

Before lessons began, they were sitting by the deserted school pond in the shadow of a long line of sunflowers being grown for the annual Fivetors and Twinhills Tallest Sunflower prize. Raven listened as Morti and Nightshade bickered without

enthusiasm. It was already too hot for them to argue seriously.

'Everyone reckons no one sits by this pond any more cos it's where Mr Pickles was found. But I reckon it's cos old Odorless pops down here about three times a day to feed something to those sunflowers,' said Morti. 'He's obsessed. His whole life is about beating Fivetors at something. He even pushes sunflowers into submission. Is it possible this Howling Hag business is all about Odorless sending us a message that if we don't win something soon, we all get cursed? If he could use magic to get us to win something, he'd do it.'

Nightshade lifted her pink nose in the air. 'Fish guts. Think he's using that as a fertilizer. Not magic.'

For Raven, there was little worse than imagining blustering, bullying Mr Odorless being the secret sorcerer. She had read too much about the sort of things that happened when angry, ambitious people like Mr Odorless discovered magic. Even imagining him discovering Rookery's true talent was terrifying. She could picture him rubbing his thin white hands together.

'Fish guts! Bleurgh! Even in the tallest sunflower battle, competition is very high,' said Morti. He picked up a small stone and tossed it into the pond with a tiny plop. 'Your school has the most ridiculous competitions.'

'It's your school now,' said Raven.

'Yeah, till Mum and Dad haul me off somewhere else.' Morti lobbed another stone into the pond, a bigger one that made a satisfying plop. 'Odorless is too good a suspect to abandon just cos we didn't find any evidence.'

'I think the general idea of being a detective is that is exactly what you do,' said Nightshade.

Raven had nothing to report back either. She worried she might have spotted more and got the evidence they needed against Mr Odorless, if she had been brave enough to do the breaking and entering.

'What about hunches?' Morti rolled over and dug in his pocket for snacks, then broke off a long piece of grass to chew on. 'All detectives have hunches. My hunch was we should have started with the murder of Mr Pickles. Those scissors in his belly – might have been a clear warning of what can happen if we let old Odorless down. And Mr Pickles made everyone laugh at him.'

'That's your idea of a motive, is it?' Nightshade asked, rolling on to her side to begin a big all-over wash. 'That he's trying to terrify everyone into beating Fivetors?'

Morti demanded to know more about magic. Nightshade explained sorcerers tended to be best at a particular kind of magic. But once you discovered your natural talents, you studied to develop skills in different kinds of magic. It could take years of practice. And magic brought power, but also responsibility.

'Thought it'd be more exciting than that,' said Morti. 'So you read books and study magic, and you just wait? And don't know if you will even get magic?'

The way he said it suggested Raven's whole way of life was strange. Everything seemed to confirm that life would be a whole lot easier without magic. People assumed if they were magical they could do anything, or at the very least, it would be pretty fun. When Morti had thought he could understand animals he had been beyond thrilled.

'You need to study because when magical folk meet with terrible ends, it's usually through lack of skill with their magic,' she tried to explain, thinking of Snapdragon's own magical tragedy. And Snapdragon had been very skilled.

'True. If magic goes bad, it's usually by mistake. Few sorcerers or witches set out to be evil,' said Nightshade. 'Not like this curse we're dealing with.'

Morti asked for an example, so Nightshade told him the story of Mortuary Catkin, who had been able to conjure such strong firebolts with his fingers he could bend metal with his bare hands and had got a job as a blacksmith.

'. . . He made such beautiful weather vanes and twirly gates and got rather rich and very popular and only wanted to use magic for good. But he burnt down an entire hotel. All he meant to do was to show off by lighting a candle at the start of a romantic meal with someone he wanted to impress.'

Morti listened carefully. 'So Mortuary is a magical name. P'raps I should call myself Mortuary.'

Raven explained that a mortuary was not somewhere you'd want to be too associated with.

'Are you just waiting too, Morti Scratch?' said Nightshade lazily. 'Or do you have an idea of what you want to be?'

Morti let out a big sigh. 'I always thought – a detective. But you'd think it would be easier than this, wouldn't you?'

'It's never easier than this.'

Morti's eyes grew rounder. 'Have your cases always been this tricky?'

'Trickier,' answered Nightshade, polishing her whiskers.

'You really are some sort of Sherlock Holmes cat, aren't you? You walk the mean streets of the magical world.'

'I've been up against some very ruthless criminals. It is particularly easy to evade detection when you use magic to commit a crime. We need to be alert at all times. We didn't call it Operation Optimistic.' Nightshade tucked her legs beneath her; her ears and whiskers twitched. A tiny blue bird had alighted near the pond.

'Please don't kill anything right in front of me,' Raven pleaded.

'So, what you are saying is I had to go through that hell so we could investigate Mr Odorless and we got nothing,' said Morti, returning to his earlier grumbling.

'What hell did you go through?' asked Nightshade. 'It was me who actually broke into Tidy House.'

'And failed to locate the crucial evidence. My hell was spending time with that mutt,' said Morti with a shudder. 'You don't like the teeth, I get that. It's the slobber that gets me. That and the wheezing. Honestly, keeping Titus going to give you long enough to search was a nightmare. Dogs who don't like walks aren't really dogs, are they? I kept thinking

I should call an ambulance. And I tried to squeeze the kid for answers, but Carsen saw nothing that break time, unless he'd worked out I'm collecting intel and lied,' said Morti gloomily. 'I do think he's hiding something. We need a breakthrough if we're going to crack this case.'

Morti offered around some cherry lollies that Mr Odorless would confiscate if he got so much as a sniff of. Nightshade shook her head, but Raven accepted one nervously. All sweets were utterly banned from Twinhills and just watching Morti eating one so openly made her glance around. She wouldn't be surprised if Mr Odorless could smell them all the way from his office.

Morti spoke thickly as he rolled the cherry lollipop around in his mouth. 'OK, we've given updates on Operation Pickles Primary Phase. You're next, Raven.'

'Thought it was Alpha Phase,' muttered Night-shade.

'Tell us the Howling Hag's story. Why's she returned to wreak some sort of revenge on the school? Or her ancestors have?'

'I couldn't find anything,' Raven answered in a small voice.

The only discovery she had made was that terrifying mask. And she had no intention of mentioning that, certainly not until she'd had a chance to get some answers out of Rookery. Because that mask made her sister look guilty of something, only she didn't know what. Just something horrible. Why might her sister be hiding such a vile thing? A fancy dress party, a play? Her sister was better at keeping secrets than she had ever realized. Raven was going to have to get better at digging them out. Finding that mask had changed everything. She had to find a way to talk to her sister, because it really looked as if Rookery was involved in something.

'I say park the Howling Hag for now. It's time to move into Operation Pickles Secondary Phase,' said Morti.

'I didn't realize we had a Secondary Phase,' said Raven.

Morti was looking at Raven expectantly. 'Not us – you. I've grilled one suspect, Nightshade breached an enemy lair. Now it's your chance to infiltrate. You need to go covert. First break time is the perfect chance to investigate and gather intel. Next target: Suspect Aaliyah.'

16. OPERATION PICKLES – SECONDARY PHASE

There were hundreds of daisies invitingly scattered across the school grounds. *I could sit and make a wonderful daisy chain*, thought Raven. Instead, she found herself sighing, with no choice but to head to the dark indoors of Miss Percy's classroom with its heady smell of paint in search of Aaliyah, and in the hope, but little expectation, of clues.

This is what happened when you took advice from a talking cat.

Raven popped her head around the door into

Miss Percy's classroom and there was Aaliyah, busy tidying pots and pencils as usual. Raven asked cheerily if she needed a hand, resigning herself to wasting her entire break arranging the big squeezy paints under Aaliyah's forensic eye.

Aaliyah was tiny, and with big puppy-dog eyes, more like someone you'd sneak into your pocket than someone who'd terrify the whole school with bad magic. She never went anywhere without a small woolly bag with mournful eyes, so it looked like she was tailed by a very sad, very shaggy sheep.

'Oh, I can manage fine by myself.' The girl turned, her look less than welcoming. She switched to a new task.

'Rearranging the pictures, what a good idea,' said Raven. 'I'd love to do that.'

Nightshade insisted that getting on the trail of whoever had got into Miss Percy's locked box without being seen was key to getting them close to unmasking the Howling Hag. The talking cat had said it was a matter of finding out people's secrets and knowing which ones were important. But Aaliyah? Hard to imagine she had something dangerous concealed in the mournful sheep bag, or that she tidied pencils as a cover for perfecting a sinister incantation.

So far Operation Pickles was way too much Mr Odorless, an awful lot of tricky questions and no easy way of getting answers. And the plan to get intel out of Aaliyah was going to be a challenge as she never said much at the best of times.

'It's a bit hot outside for me today,' lied Raven, moving carefully into the classroom. Aailyah may have the look of a puppy, but could show her teeth if you moved something out of a neat line.

What kind of dark secret could Aaliyah possibly have? Even Morti had said that if you were going to name one Twinhills student who always followed the rules, helped out the teachers and would never be in trouble, it was Aaliyah. Of course, according to Morti this actually made Aaliyah the best suspect (by way of being the least likely, apparently).

Raven was not convinced of the logic, but someone was practising witchcraft at Twinhills. Who genuinely did seem likely? She resigned herself to doing her best to find out what she could. She desperately needed to find a decent suspect, any alternative to Rookery. She needed to persuade Aaliyah to tell anything at all that she might know.

'This is a much better way to spend break time,' Raven said, persevering. 'How are we sorting them? By size?'

Aaliyah was still doing her best to ignore Raven. She had dark hair tied in a smooth ponytail. If ever Raven tried to get her hair to arrange itself neatly, bits escaped and flew out, determined to go their own way. She said as much to Aaliyah and this brought a smile to her serious face.

'It's as if my hair has a life of its own,' Raven went on with a grin, and took the chance to move right next to Aaliyah, who concentrated on rearranging the pictures the class had been painting in the last lesson. Miss Percy had them pegged on a line right across the classroom to dry.

Aaliyah watched Raven move another picture, fidgeting with her fingers. 'Not that one,' she corrected nervously, 'that wouldn't be right. Alphabetically.'

'Great!' said Raven with enthusiasm, taking down the picture she had just done, checking the name written on the back and moving it. 'I like tidying.'

She was rewarded with a shy smile. 'I prefer it to going outside to play those kind of make-up games that people do at break time,' Aaliyah confessed.

Raven gently took a couple of pegs from Aaliyah, who was struggling, holding the pegs awkwardly. She felt a flash of understanding that if you were Aaliyah, life made so much more sense if you arranged things well.

'You are so good at this,' Raven said with a big smile. 'This will make it so much easier for Miss Percy to hand them out later.'

Raven knew some people (Sam Carruthers especially) could be scathing about Aaliyah's eccentricities. Sam had the biggest muscles of anyone at the school and was best at every single one of the sports, so could always get a laugh, even when being a little cruel at someone else's expense.

Aaliyah really was holding the pegs awkwardly and Raven noticed on her fingers were two plasters.

'Is that painful?' Raven swooped in to hang the next picture.

Aaliyah just looked even more uncomfortable, pulling around her ponytail, which was long enough so that she could chew the end.

'Shall we do paints next?' suggested Raven. 'Do you do them alphabetically too?'

Aaliyah threw Raven a withering look. 'No! That would be stupid. The colours get sorted by colours of the rainbow. You know, red first, then orange—'

'Yes.' Raven could not stop herself responding tartly, then added more gently, 'It's more complicated than I'd realized. But,' she repeated, 'you are very good at it.'

Aaliyah gave a conspiratorial smile. 'I just do what seems right.' Aaliyah flinched as she tried to peg another picture and Raven insisted on taking the rest of the pegs. When she put up the next picture, she received a nod of approval.

'I sort my biscuits into size at home,' said Aaliyah.

'That *is* a good idea,' said Raven. 'Although in our house biscuits never last very long anyway. Do you like biscuits?'

'Doesn't everyone like biscuits?'

It was no good standing here waffling on about biscuits. Break time would be over soon. The whole point was to find out what Aaliyah had seen. And as Raven tried to muster the courage to steer the conversation, suddenly she could see how crucial it was to get Aaliyah to talk. Because Aaliyah spent all her breaks tidying. That meant she must have been here when the money and the stone vanished. Surely it would be impossible for someone to have slipped in here, unlocked the box somehow, stolen the money and the stone, and put it all back undisturbed, all without Aaliyah seeing something. There was a high chance she had actually seen the Howling Hag get close enough to perform some sort of magic to get into that locked box. Who was it?

Aaliyah could be key to unlocking the whole mystery.

'Your fingers really do look painful, I'm glad I

could help.' Raven was desperately trying to work up to a way to get Aailayh to trust her enough to talk. Aaliyah stared at the two big plasters on her fingers and said they didn't hurt any more and chewed furiously on her ponytail.

'How did you hurt them?' Raven asked kindly.

Quite a lot of the children seemed to be wearing plasters for hurt fingers, but now Raven had asked about them, Aaliyah's face took on the woeful, guilty look of a dog who was very, very sorry for pinching the sausages.

Of all the things Raven might have asked, offering sympathy for hurt fingers was clearly completely wrong. Because one second Aliyah was becoming friendly, chatting about biscuits and pointing exactly where Raven should hang the last of the pictures, then she blurted out: 'I didn't empty Miss Percy's secret box. I haven't got the money and the stone. I wouldn't.'

'No, well, I'm sure . . .' Raven felt confused. 'No one's saying you did.'

Aaliyah was trembling.

'But you were here in the classroom the break time when they were stolen. You might have seen something important?' Raven pressed, as gently as she could. 'It would be a big help.'

Aaliyah's frightened puppy-dog eyes grew wider. She touched her injured fingers on the small woolly sheep-shaped bag and drew it close to her chest.

'Please Aaliyah – what did you see? Something that scared you?'

Aaliyah simply stood there, clutching the sheep bag.

'Was someone in here?' Raven tried, before she lost this chance completely. 'Did something strange happen?'

Aaliyah shook her head in the tiniest motion. 'No, no, that's not how it works,' she whispered

Raven wished she knew the right thing to say next. 'Well, how does it work? Was it Mr Odorless?' she tried. 'Is that why you're frightened?'

But it was too much for Aaliyah. Squeezing and squeezing at the sheep bag, she said: 'I haven't got anything to hide.' Then she turned and fled.

Raven stared after her. She had come into this classroom with very little expectation, but she felt she was on the edge of . . . something, she just wasn't sure what it was.

Aaliyah had claimed she wasn't hiding anything, yet she was holding on to her sheep satchel like her life depended on it. Maybe she was hiding something. Raven knew she had to see inside that bag. The trouble was, Aaliyah never let it out of her sight.

17. THE DEATH OF *NIGHT SKY*

Morti almost forgot to eat his lunchtime pasta he was so enthralled by Raven's report. She tried not to leave out any detail, however small. From the strange comment Aaliyah made, *that's not how it works*, to her suspicions the girl was hiding something and it was lurking in that fluffy sheep-shaped bag; even the odd thing about the plasters.

'Operation Pickles Secondary Phase critical success! Brilliant, Raven. We can move to Operation Pickles, Secondary Phase, Extension Mode.' Morti

moved on to prodding cautiously in his plastic dessert cup. 'What is this epic green nastiness we are expected to eat?'

Raven sighed. 'VGJ days seem to come around far more quickly than butterscotch delight or sponge pudding and custard days.'

'VGJ?'

'Vile Green Jelly. No one eats it, not since Carsen Samuels said it's mushed leftover vegetables – Mr Odorless's latest brain-boosting wheeze to beat Fivetors in exams.'

Morti hurriedly put down the pot. 'Well, nearly time for us to join Miss Percy's class and get out of this prison. Can't wait for our afternoon of freedom. Bring on the den building and campfires. Last time she brought us all school egg sandwiches as well.'

They watched Sam Carruthers lazily pick up a leftover apple and orange from the lunchtime fresh fruit and begin to juggle slowly. Ella giggled and tossed him a banana as well. This he caught effortlessly and then kept three fruits moving and started to draw a crowd. Carsen Samuels reached in and swiped the banana and somehow it became a game of catch right across the school hall.

'It'll be a doddle, you getting a look in that bag,' Morti said thoughtfully, clearly unwilling to let Raven forget Operation Pickles even for a moment. 'All you have to do is sneak into the cloakroom while Aaliyah's in PE, playing netball, tennis, whatever. Even Aaliyah can't keep the mournful sheep for PE.'

'Tennis and cricket,' Raven replied absent-mindedly because she was fixating on the comment 'all you have to do'.

'Exactly.'

The level of giggling and laughing grew as Sam and Carsen got further and further apart, throwing the fruit almost from one end of the school hall to the other. Sam dodged easily out of the way of a dinner lady who failed to stop him.

One apple smashed on the floor in a mush of pulp and pips after a bad miss from Carsen. Everyone groaned and Aaliyah shyly threw him another.

An orange whopped Misha on the side of the head when he tried to join in and Carsen's brother, Jackson, kept trying to dive in and catch one of the pieces of fruit, but it was all flying too high and too fast.

Then a crash and a splintering of glass put a stop to the fruit game. Every head turned. Raven and Morti were on their feet. What had happened? A couple of the younger kids let up a wail.

'Did some of the flying fruit hit something?' Morti wondered aloud.

But it was in a corner, far from the fruit game, where the wailing was coming from. Raven could see that several of the upset children were sprinkled with glistening slivers of glass. Rookery and Bianca moved over to help. Ella went across and bent down to pick up something from the floor, shaking her head. Her face was tense as she handed something to Henry Figgins, something broken, just as Miss Percy arrived to take charge.

'It's Henry's picture. *Night Sky*!' breathed Morti, craning his neck.

Then the muttering began, first quiet and gentle, then like the breath of a monster on the back of your neck: *The Howling Hag!*

Raven stared around wildly. How had Henry's picture fallen from the display of the Twinhills Photography Club competition?

Raven looked to where the other winners were still displayed. Bianca's cute picture of Lady McFluff, *Stylish Hamster*, proudly showed a 'second place' certificate. Carsen had been awarded third place for a close-up action shot of his brother – *Goal!*

Beneath where Henry's first-prize winning *Night Sky* had been in pride of place, the floor was showered with broken glass. Sam Carruthers fetched a broom and started to sweep up, as the chanting grew.

She's going to trick you. She's going to get you. She's going to eat you.

'Magic,' said Morti. 'Has to be. The only people near that picture were those tinies who got covered in glass. But who was it? She did her magic right here and I didn't see anything!'

Raven couldn't help but find her gaze drawn to her sister.

Everyone crowded in to sympathize with Henry, but Raven felt frozen, remembering that spat between Rookery and Henry, the dirty water spilt over Rookery's best-ever picture, the paint that had ended up on Henry's shirt just before he'd been presented with his prize certificate for that photograph.

Bianca said loudly that her mum would get busy with the first aid box and she and Rookery ushered out anyone who had been sprinkled with shattered glass.

Raven knew Rookery's eyes turned from yellowish and catlike to ever so slightly smoky if she was doing magic. But Raven couldn't make out any signs.

Miss Percy had arrived and gently took the shattered wreckage of the picture Henry had been so proud of from his trembling fingers. All that was left was a smashed frame, his photograph ripped.

'I'm so sorry, Henry,' Miss Percy said. 'It looks as if it must have fallen. I'm sure it can be fixed.'

Miss Sunny arrived too and Miss Percy briskly announced it was time to head outside for her forest lesson, but had her work cut out getting everyone to stop focusing on the unsettling events.

Morti began immediately: 'Didn't Nightshade say to do magic you have to be near? Where were our suspects? Rookery, Bianca, Carsen and Aaliyah were all here. Shame old Odorless wasn't,' said Morti. 'Guess we really do have to rule him out. And Miss Percy and Miss Sunny weren't either. Maybe Nightshade's idea that they were all our best suspects wasn't as right as she thought.'

Raven simply had no idea what to think. Apart from the very unwelcome thought that getting something to move with just her mind was exactly the magic Rookery was very skilled at . . .

Maybe Morti was guessing her thoughts, because she felt his hand reassuringly placed on her shoulder to steer her outside to the survival lesson. 'Let's go join 'em. And don't worry, Raven. We are heading to Tertiary Phase of Operation Pickles. If anything can solve it, that can.'

18. Getting Her Sister To Talk

Raven arrived home full of determination to talk to Rookery, but she was confronted with Mum, wobbling precariously on a stool. Her desk was pushed right up against the wall and the carpet rolled back into an untidy mound in front of the entrance to the secret compartment. There was a distinct smell that candles had been burning. And all across the wooden floor where the carpet had lain, there were scribbled symbols and sigils in chalk.

'There's Knox's fresh lemonade in the fridge,'

Mum trilled with a distracted wave.

In the middle of the chalk scribblings was a tiny silver teaspoon. Raven guessed Mum still hadn't broken the curse that had turned someone's silver into chocolate.

The Charmings were never going to hide these signs of magical goings-on in a hurry. Raven only hoped Rookery wouldn't choose today to bring Bianca home again.

All she really wanted was a thick slice of jam on toast, as she often did when she got in from school. But all the drawers and cupboards in the kitchen were open and empty. She groaned and thought what an utterly terrible day it had been. She wasn't sure which bit had been the worst. Even Miss Percy's bushcraft lessons had to be abandoned – for the second week in a row. The gate to the woods had refused to open, the lock completely stuck fast even in the face of Miss Percy's determination.

And the chanting had begun. Raven could feel it – see the nervous glancing over shoulders. All the children suspected the Howling Hag of being up to her tricks again, spoiling even more of their fun. Mr Odorless had scuttled out of this office to join in with unhelpful comments while slurping coffee from his World's Best Head Teacher mug and hit them with an outdoors spelling test. Miss Percy looked as if she might try to blow the gate off its hinges. Everything was now put down to the Howling Hag and her evil curses.

Raven had nothing to scoop out any jam with except an old plastic spoon (which she gave a quick wipe first). She gave up on the butter.

How could she persuade Rookery to talk and share what she knew?

A sound from upstairs told her Rookery was home earlier than usual. This might be her chance, if she could just get up the courage to do what Morti would probably call *grill her sister*. Raven gingerly poked her head around the door to her sister's room, wondering why Rookery was skulking there. Had she had a row with Bianca?

Raven asked if she wanted bread and jam. She didn't even get to explaining about the butter.

Rookery slammed the door.

Raven stared at the closed door. There was so much she wanted to say. Are you in trouble, Rookery? Is there some dark reason why suddenly magic is spilling out of you that brings tricks and unkindness? Has the Howling Hag got some sort of hold on you? Why have you got a horrible mask? Rookery – did you kill Mr Pickles?

It was difficult even to imagine that conversation and she slunk quietly back downstairs. As well as she thought she knew her sister, there was no getting away from the fact that something was troubling Rookery and it had to be something to do with the upsurge in magic in Twinhills and that horrible mask.

Mum, precarious on the stool, was concentrating. 'Sorry about the cutlery,' she said. 'I couldn't risk turning any silver we had into chocolate and I thought I'd be on the safe side and remove all the metal from the house. It's all in a big basket under the apple tree. But don't worry about the kitchen, because . . .' Her voice faded and her expression changed.

Then she leapt off the stool and announced that they were due up at Knox's for dinner. She yelled for Rookery and they found themselves hustled out of the door.

Mum was soon leading them briskly past Tidy House where Mr Odorless was busy spraying his flowers with something to make all insects within a ten-metre radius drop down dead. Mum plunged them into the woods, saying they'd take the shortcut. She'd given such an anxious glance at Tidy House Raven wondered if the grouchy old head could be part of the reason why Mum had sent them to Fivetors school before Twinhills.

149

Rookery dragged her feet, slipping further and further behind, as if going to Knox's was the worst punishment in the world. She had the same face as when she'd opened the biscuit tin and Raven had to explain that Morti had finished every last one of the chocolate biscuits.

Every time there was the smallest of rustlings in the undergrowth, Rookery gave a shriek and made a startled move.

The three took the path that swung around the back of the school, towards the clearing with the hanging tree and the remains of the Howling Hag's fire. Was it possible that fire was being used by one of her descendants to conjure up bad magic? There were so many unanswered questions.

Raven reminded herself it wasn't possible for the Howling Hag to have returned. But she could not stop herself looking around fearfully, half expecting to see a pointed hat in the undergrowth or a broomstick in the shadows.

This is nonsense, she told herself. But her heart was not listening. It was pounding as if she'd run all the way here.

Raven looked back to where her sister lagged behind. A group of birds flew upwards and Rookery jumped as if a monster had appeared on the path.

She tried to hang back to talk to her sister, but Mum was suddenly alongside her, saying brightly: 'How are things going, Raven?'

And that just made Raven's spirits sink lower, and that dark little hole inside her woke up again. Neg took the chance to grow as she tried to find an equally cheery way of replying, because she knew what Mum was really asking, because it was what Mum always meant – *Any signs of that magic yet?*

It reminded Raven of how many secrets she was keeping, because right now, her lack of magic wasn't even the worst problem in her life.

They passed the hanging tree, with its unpleasant name, dubious associations, and definitely bad memories for her family. Suddenly everything about Twinhills, about Beechy Wood, everything, felt weighed down with history and stories and expectation. All Mum's books ever taught her was how magic made bad things happen.

'Mum, why do we live in Twinhills among people who don't believe in magic?' Raven asked, surprising herself. 'Rookery has to work hard all the time not to do magic.'

'Ours is a complicated family,' Mum sighed. A typical Mum answer. The sort she always delivered, always with a smile, saying it was just that their challenges were a little different to most people's: *We have enough money for our bills, none of us is ill and we all love each other. We're at our best when we work together.* What she meant, of course, was that the most crucial thing about their lives was something that had to stay secret.

'Did you send us to Fivetors first and not Twin-hills only because you thought there was less chance Rookery would stand out for being so magical?'

Or did Mum suspect horrible Mr Odorless was a descendant of a sorcerer and might have the power to use magic for bad things?

'I did hope she wouldn't get noticed, plus Snapdragon always felt the head teacher had bad feelings towards magic, unfortunately.'

'Bad feelings about magic? Snapdragon wanted to keep us away from Mr Odorless because he knows about magic?'

Mum sighed. 'The trouble with my job is that you see the worst side of magic. I break curses because people have used magic wrongly and usually it's because they are either greedy or lazy, most usually both. Or they wouldn't be using magic for the wrong things in the first place.'

It sounded very much as if Mr Odorless had been involved in some sort of magic. But before Raven had chance to get more answers out of Mum, there was a tremendous rustling and a flurry of startled birds. What had startled them? She glanced about, but Rookery was calling from a long way back that she was feeling ill and just wanted to be at home. Without waiting for any response, she swung around, plunged back, heading the opposite way. Within seconds she was swallowed up by the wood, as invisible as if she had never been there at all.

Mum stared after her, her face creased with worry. 'I knew something was up. I should go with her.' She glanced at Raven and then at the path ahead. 'Now, you don't have to miss out on the trip to Knox's. It's not far . . . are you all right to carry on by yourself?'

Raven heard herself take a big gulp. Her head snapped around at the swish of rustling in the shrubby undergrowth, the exact sound of someone lurking and creepily following. She had to ignore that little hollowed-out dark hole and show Neg who was boss, because Mum was right – Rookery needed Mum more right now. And she was pleased Mum trusted her to be old enough to do this last bit. It wasn't far. Even on her own, she could do this.

She concentrated on being excited about Knox's and pressed on hurriedly. But she could not quite resist turning, telling herself she was only going to wave, yet hoping Mum might have changed her mind and might be hurrying after her. But Mum was gone, not so much as a sway of grass showing where she had vanished into the trees. As if Beechy Wood had eaten her up.

Raven tried to put a bounce in her step. She loved these woods. She loved Grandpa Knox's. With Knox, magic was always fun. Knox could be relied on to entertain her with at least one spell he was supposed to keep secret. Yes, think about Knox's. Think about that brilliant old kettle that Snapdragon had charmed. It poured out whatever you needed most. You could guarantee hot chocolate in the winter. Or a thick tomato soup. If you concentrated really hard you could get some cheesy garlic bread croutons floating in it. Today she'd ask for iced lemonade. Unlimited iced lemonade from Snapdragon's kettle. That's what she needed to think about, not about looking too deeply into the woods and spotting the Howling Hag. *No. She is not going to make you afraid. She has not come back from the dead. You know that is nonsense.*

There was rustling. Definitely rustling. She did not turn.

Think of something else.

Building sandcastles on the kitchen floor. Yes!

She'd discovered the kettle could easily pour entire buckets of sand. Once, when a visiting dog had fleas, Snapdragon had poured out a measure of some foul-smelling thick liquid that had sent the fleas (and everyone else) hopping. Twice Raven had asked for a potion to make her hair turn black and smooth. The first time nothing had poured out at all. The second time she had lifted the lid and discovered two chocolate biscuits. It had almost been as if she'd been able to hear Snapdragon whispering, *Magic isn't supposed to solve all your problems.*

More than a gentle rustling.

More as if something was moving alongside her, keeping pace with her under cover of the tall grasses. She tried to swallow but her mouth was too dry. She started to hurry.

A rustling – definitely. Someone was there. Raven began to run.

Not far to Knox's. Not far to the edge of the woods. She could see where the trees ended and the sunlight dappled ahead as her feet sped, quickly reaching a rhythmical thundering on the path. She didn't dare turn, she could feel her chest starting to hurt, her legs protest, but she daren't stop because the bracken was bending in time with her and someone was moving alongside.

19. A SECRET SPELL?

I landed on the path right in front of her and Raven screamed. I had an undignified leaf attached to my nose; I knew because it was so big I could see it. I might have looked a bit like the bushes springing to life – I'd had to wrench myself out of some particularly prickly undergrowth. But scream?

Seriously? Yet there was something about Raven's terrified look that made me turn slowly, heart beating at a pace, scouring the trees for something behind me.

'Nightshade! It's only you!' Raven breathed. She bent down to kindly remove a few prickles of green attached to my fur. 'I thought . . .' She shook her head. 'Why were you sneaking along like that?'

'She keeps getting way too close with that intrusive instrument of hers. I'm getting the evils every time she sees me.'

'Mum? You were brave enough to break into Mr Odorless's house, but you ran away from the bracelet Mum uses to investigate magic?' Raven smiled down at me. 'I don't think it's an evil look. You said you were on holiday in Twinhills, but you never said how come you can talk. But that's magic, isn't it, and I bet Mum senses there's something magical about you – she's pretty good at spotting stuff like that.'

'Well, the last thing I need is the Grand High Inquisitor.' In seconds we were out of the sinister trees, where barely a sunbeam danced, and out on to the sun-bleached edges where the sun hurt your eyes.

'She could cure you, you know.'

'Cure me?'

'Well, I'm guessing it's not easy making friends when you're the only cat who can talk. And you can't let on to humans either. Isn't it lonely?'

'About as tough as having a sister who is so effortlessly magic it spills out of her, giving her the world's biggest secret to keep, now with the added trouble of a fancy non-magical best friend.'

Raven gave me a closed-face look. It's true. I actually have no idea how I can talk, but I wouldn't swap my problems for Raven Charming's.

We were almost at Knox's and young Raven had definitely lost her chirpiness. 'You don't think I'm magical, do you?' she said, stalking ahead in what I was quick to interpret as a decidedly frosty manner. 'You may as well come out and say it. It's what everyone thinks. But no one ever says.'

I had to scamper in all this heat to keep up with her. I'd said the wrong thing. Well, she started it. Cure me indeed! 'You mustn't give up magic, you know,' I said. 'Have you tried—'

'I think I must have tried everything, thank you, Nightshade.'

'I'm just saying, magic can be a right pain. Half the time it doesn't follow rules anyone can understand. You're probably just a little choked. Your natural magic might flood out any time – if you were in danger, for example.'

'Choked?' Raven stopped, drew herself up and put as much indignation into the word as if I'd accused her of murdering Mr Pickles. 'So, your suggestion is to, let's say, summon a big monster to scare my magic into waking up. So, what if my affinity is for seeing? My magic would kick in just in time so I'd get a really good idea of exactly how nastily I was going to get eaten.'

'It was only a suggestion.'

The path got steeper as we closed in on Dandelion Cottage.

'I'm just saying I understand it can't be easy having a grandma who died when her magic went wrong. Nor having a sister like Rookery. Look at me – I can't do any magic. You can still be a good and useful person.'

'Cat.'

'Yes.'

She was still bristling as effectively as if she had fur. So I told her how glad I was to have met her and Morti. Not that I was pleased that there was something wicked going on at the school. But it had brought us together. And she was right, magic certainly makes you feel different. It can be lonely.

'I guess you are missing your . . . Do you have a human?' she said.

'He prefers to be called Seth,' I answered. I explained he was all tied up in something where there was no place for me. 'Talking is good. I hope your sister has got someone to talk to. She seems worried.'

My suspicion was that Raven knew something she didn't want to share. I guessed it was about her sister. And I knew I'd somehow messed up this chance I'd had to get her to open up to me, because we were at Knox's.

Sorcerers never know what sort of weird tales people might spin when they approach you to ask for a little magical help; they learn to hide their shock. Well, most do...

Knox looked so startled when we walked through the door, he began to stir his tea with the remains of a jam tart he was munching. 'You're here for dinner? What's the time?' He looked down at me. 'And you have brought this lovely cat with you.' He delved through a jumble of tins next to a gaudy umbrella stand and extracted an old and dented one. He removed the lid, revealing a giant plateful of chocolate and caramel biscuits. 'Will these do?'

Raven bucked up immediately. I looked up at him and purred.

'I think that means she'd like some milk,' said Raven.

I miaowed and gave Raven the big eyes.

'And a piece of salmon, but only if you have one. Any kind of fish will do.'

I pawed at Raven's leg.

'And a jam tart if you have any left.'

The training was really paying off.

'I'm not sure that cat should have jam tarts.' Knox seated himself across the kitchen table from Raven, while I got the floor, which I was used to.

'Oh, I'm pretty sure that cat does lots of things she's not supposed to.'

She gave me a conspiratorial smile, which dropped the instant Knox said: 'Did Snapdragon show you her magical preparation that keeps spiders out of cupboards? It's very simple. We could try it together, now you're here.'

'I followed that spell to the letter,' said Raven, her face closed and tense. 'We put my spell in the darkest corner of the shed and a spider ran right over it. In fact, I'm pretty sure it stopped and lifted up one of its legs to wave at me.'

'Ah well, magical preparations are not everyone's cup of tea. Or maybe it's silver,' said Knox, going off on one of his tangents as he rummaged in a canister near the stove and unearthed a jam tart, which he dropped on to a plate on the floor for me. 'There was this interesting case. Someone had been slipped a silver horseshoe to carry for good luck, only the silver blocked his magic.'

'Well, silver is definitely not blocking my magic –

every bit of metal in the house is currently in a basket in the back garden.'

Knox began to tell a story about one poor witch, Bertha Gumm, whose only magical skill was to blow bubbles. '... But she got so good at it by the time she was seven she could join bubbles together and make any animal you cared to mention. By the time she was twenty-three she had risen from being a huge hit at children's parties to playing to sold-out audiences at the Sydney Opera House, of which she made a bubble replica as her grand finale.'

I knew exactly what Knox was doing. He was trying to be helpful, pointing out that magic could fall entirely at random and that you just had to accept whatever magic you might discover you had and make the most of it.

But I knew Raven did not need to hear it now. I picked up the jam tart and took it out to the front doorstep, giving Raven the big old eyes. She was getting good at interpreting, and moments later sank gratefully on to the front doorstep next to me, heaving a great big sigh the moment Knox was out of earshot.

'Even bubble-blowing Bertha knew her affinity before she was seven,' she sighed, nudging me along the step a bit.

I had questions for her, before we got interrupted. 'You found something in the Howling Hag's fire the other day. Care to share what it was?'

I thought she was going to avoid answering, but she put her hand in her pocket and pulled out a singed piece of paper. 'Can you read, Nightshade?' It was just a scrap, scorched and badly burnt, but you could just about make out words written on it. Or, at least, letters.

'Read? Of course I can read! But maybe you can tell me what you think it says.' When she read it out, I had no clue what it meant.

orld's Best Headte
ash i
mber Mr Pi

'Could it be the remains of a spell?' I hazarded. 'One that was burnt in the fire? Do you recognize what sort of magic that might be?'

Raven answered with a very big and weary sigh and a shake of her head. Her face was all creased up and I reminded her to have more lemonade. 'I keep thinking if only I knew what magic was being used . . .'

'Well, I think this helps,' I said gently. 'I think this tells us it's unlikely this is down to Rookery,' I reassured her. 'Because Rookery's magic doesn't need spells and cauldrons and standing around fires. If this is a spell, surely that points to it not being Rookery being behind the curses.'

Then it all came out. She confessed about the horrible discovery of a scary mask her sister had hidden away. I knew she was convinced Rookery was involved in something bad. There are times when being able to speak is no help at all. I put my head in her lap and I knew that was the right thing to do when she started rubbing my ears.

'She's in trouble, Nightshade,' she said. 'I just don't know what sort.'

Then she muttered something in a whisper. She seemed to be picking up the rest of her family's habit of thoughts not necessarily following an obvious trail. Because I thought what she said was that she needed to talk to Snapdragon.

Which was impossible, because Snapdragon was dead.

PART THREE

20. The Secret of Snapdragon

T o Raven, talking to Snapdragon seemed the only way forward. Yet it was something she knew she really shouldn't do.

The next morning she'd put on her best innocent face and said that Knox wasn't teaching his yoga class in the village hall today right after school, so she was heading up to Dandelion Cottage. Which meant Mum could go to that work meeting she'd mentioned if she wanted to.

Mum had looked up from her desk and put one of

the ends of her glasses in her mouth. And agreed right away, which made Raven feel bad as Mum really was super busy. Should she be pleased she was getting so good at deception?

But the only way to be sure no one in her family found out about her speaking to her dead grandmother was to tell a lie. Actually, quite a few lies.

She didn't like sneaking into an empty Dandelion Cottage, but she'd got involved with Operation Pickles to protect Rookery and keep the magical world a secret. And so far, everything had just got more and more muddled. How did the Howling Hag play her tricks so cleverly? The curses might have started out small. But killing Mr Pickles had scared and upset everyone. Making that picture crash in a packed hall had been daring. But even in a room full of people, no one had seen anything. The Howling Hag's power was growing.

But Raven had failed to even discover anything about her or why she or one of her descendants might want to target the school.

Was everything beginning to point to Rookery being involved, or possibly getting tricked into practising the wrong sort of magic? Raven was beginning to despair of where to turn next in search of answers.

She pushed open the door to the empty cottage:

unlocked as she'd suspected. She took in the welcoming, friendly smell of fresh baking and tried to enjoy it and not be overwhelmed by the guilt at lying and letting people down. It would only set off Neg, the little hollow of doubt she carried around.

Raven crept up the spiral stairs that curved around the tree trunk that grew through the centre of the cottage. She went swiftly to Grandpa Knox's surprisingly immaculate bedroom. Everything here was as tidy as it was a jumble downstairs. Shoes were polished and in a line, clothes arranged on hangers or folded in the wardrobe. His exorbitant assortment of colourful bow ties was arranged by the colours of the rainbow. Raven thought Aaliyah would be pleased to see that.

She approached the table alongside what had once been Snapdragon's side of the bed and her heart sank. She had risked this for nothing, because the music box she was looking for, old and beautiful, ornate with lots of little pieces of inlaid wood, was no longer there.

She tried not to panic, knowing Knox would be back from his yoga class before too long, and told herself to think. That music box was so precious. Maybe Knox hadn't the heart to look at it every day. Perhaps he had moved it. She needed to search. She needed to find it.

She stood at the top of the spiral stairs staring at the uproar of untidiness that was the rest of Dandelion Cottage and tried to remember how she had first found Snapdragon.

No one had told her it was still possible to talk to her. Knox had kept that a secret. She had never intended sneaking up the stairs that time. To be honest, she never knew what made her go into Knox's room. It was as if, somehow, Snapdragon had wanted Raven to find her, because she'd found herself with Snapdragon's precious old box in her hands, staring at a tiny sleeping figure inside.

Grandma would be extremely tired and confused by being woken, but as Raven stood quietly and listened to the creaks and groans of the cottage around her, trying to still her doubts, her fears and her worry, she felt she really had no choice but to talk to her grandmother. The more you listened, the more you became aware that the house was a part of the surrounding wood and that it grew, moved, warped, stretched and shrunk with the wind and the seasons. And then she found herself drawn downstairs to the kitchen.

She spotted a white cloth on the counter covering a low shape. When she took a peek, she found a tinned loaf of banana bread left to slowly rise. Knox would doubtless pop that into the oven when he returned from teaching his class. Then he would cut himself a slice of freshly baked bread with a thick covering of one of the twenty-four different types of jam in the kitchen. Raven knew exactly how many flavours because before she really knew what she was doing, she'd counted them as she removed them one by one from the cupboard.

Bramble. Bramble and Apple. Plum. Plum and Damson. Haw and Apple. Plum and Bramble. And right at the back of the cupboard, once all the jars were higgledy-piggledy on the kitchen table, Raven found what she was seeking.

With both hands, she took out the box, noting how it looked even older and more precious than she remembered when Snapdragon was alive. Well, properly alive.

A swift and anxious glance at the handy specolens Snapdragon had set to give off warnings of un-expected visitors told her Knox wasn't yet approaching. She hastily shoved back the assortment of home-made jams. And then she drew out a wooden seat at the kitchen table and placed the beautiful hexagonal box in front of her, so close she almost pressed her nose against it, and whispered, 'Grandma? Snapdragon?'

Nothing happened. The intricate box made of too many different kinds of wood to count sat there, keeping its secret. Around the sides were inlaid scrolls and swirls of wood, light and dark, and Raven stroked them carefully with a finger, trying to remember how she had done this before.

She lifted the box, feeling for something underneath. Careful not to tip it too much, her fingers found the key and she twisted it four times clockwise. And this set off a little tinkly version of a tune. As soon as the first notes began, Raven knew whenever she heard it, this would forever remind her of Snapdragon. Her grandmother's favourite: 'Danse Macabre' by Saint-Saëns.

The top of the hexagonal box was formed of six triangular black pieces, which now began to twitch. Raven placed the box on the table, watching. The triangles moved outwards to create a dark hollow in the centre. And from the dark space a figure began to emerge, head first, holding a yoga position and wearing a lime-green top and some very colourful leggings.

'Snapdragon!' said Raven joyfully, although not without an anxious glance at the specolens. She had to put her questions quickly.

The figure twitched, then came out of the tree

pose, stretched slowly, looked directly at Raven and gave an enormous yawn. She was no bigger than a thumb, and Raven had no idea how she had come to be here.

'Raven, my dear, it's lovely to see you,' she said, blinking. She seemed to have gone into the box without her red pointy glasses and Raven knew she was quite blind without them. 'I hope you are well.'

'Not so good,' Raven answered. Just seeing Snapdragon made the dark hole of dread and doubt she was fighting inside her shrink.

She might have asked Snapdragon how she was, but her rudimentary knowledge of this sort of incredible magic meant she didn't even know if her grandma now even counted as being properly alive. Best not to ask.

'I'm sorry to hear that,' said Snapdragon sympathetically. 'Can I help?'

Two things Raven always appreciated about her grandma. First, she tried to give you answers you understood. Second, she never assumed Raven's troubles were because her magic was slow to arrive. She was the only one who did not ask Raven regularly if her affinity had revealed itself yet. Raven had always been grateful. Her grandmother made her feel that she was allowed to have normal problems –

like worrying if your friend didn't want to spend break time with you, or how to spell 'partial' and put it in a sentence.

'I want to know everything about the Howling Hag.'

She took a deep breath and waited, expecting that hole of fear inside her to open at any moment. But for once, Neg appeared to be sleeping. Asking for help felt good.

'She sounds like a menace. Witch, is she? I don't know her.'

'But Grandma, you know all the witches. The Twinhills village inn is named after her. She might have lived a long time ago. The villagers . . . they didn't try to get rid of her and not do it well, like Nelly the Nervous? Could she have found a way to come back and cause trouble? Or maybe she had family, or descendants, someone resentful about how she was treated? Wanting revenge?'

Snapdragon put her head on one side. 'Don't call me Grandma, dear. Everyone only ever calls me Snapdragon. Now, that is a lot of questions.'

'Yes, I'm sorry. But I do really need to know all I can about her.'

Snapdragon perched on top of the pedestal in the centre of her music box in a cross-legged position that did not look very comfortable. She scratched her chin.

'The Howling Hag indeed. A Twinhills witch! Such nonsense. That hideous sign at the inn! Are people telling stories that it's named after an actual witch? Many of the stories about witches are not really true, you know.' Snapdragon was shaking her head; she even looked on the edge of a chuckle. 'Raven, I don't have to tell you no real witch would ever look like that sign.'

Of course Raven knew this. Hadn't she told Morti enough times?

'And coming back for revenge?' Snapdragon scoffed. Raven could only dream of making her scoffs even half as good as Snapdragon's. That seemed to be all her grandmother was going to say on the subject.

'There's really no legend about the Howling Hag?' Raven pressed. 'You're sure?'

'I am sure no such witch ever lived in Twinhills. Until about five years ago the inn was called the Red Lion. Perfectly decent name. It's very bad luck to change a pub name, but these silly new owners ignored that tradition. Thought it was funny or clever to make something of the fact that there have always been one or two little rumours about witches being active in Twinhills.' Her smile grew broader. 'The owners came up with that silly new name and put up that horrible sign. For all the good it did them. They moved on about a year after.'

Raven had assumed Mum and Knox were being forgetful when they'd said that the Howling Hag had never been a witch working around here. Hadn't it always seemed unlikely there were two magical families based in Twinhills? But if there was no ancestor exacting revenge . . . well, someone was cursing the school. It should have been good news, but all it did was reignite Raven's fears about her sister. There *was* only one family of witches in Twinhills. Didn't that mean Rookery *had* to be involved in all the bad luck and mayhem at school?

Snapdragon moved a little closer, giving what Raven thought was supposed to be a reassuring smile. 'I am sure there is no old witch by that name. And you're right. I would know.'

'But she – *someone* is cursing our school.'

'Hmm. Sounds to me most likely someone is putting about stories to shift the blame. People are surprisingly willing to believe stories and rumours. Curses? What sort of curses? It does sound serious, Raven. You really should talk to your mother, you know. How is it going at Twinhills? Does that naughty boy Tony still live in Tidy House? I do hope he's proving to be a decent head teacher. I always felt bad that I wasn't able to do anything for him when he came to me for help.'

Despite all her worries tumbling in, Raven could not help but be surprised at this very unexpected news. 'He came to you for help? What sort of help?' The very idea of Mr Odorless consulting a witch, particularly her own grandmother, was incredible.

Snapdragon began the most enormous yawn, and at just the same time Raven saw Knox approaching in the specolens. She knew the conversation had to end, but she had not nearly got to the end of her questions.

'Thank you, Snapdragon,' said Raven, watching her grandma get into a more comfortable position to nod back to sleep. As the pedestal began to slip back inside the music box and the six triangles began to twitch and slide into place over the top, she just caught Snapdragon's last words.

'I've seen it too many times, I told him. Witchcraft is witchcraft. But no good whatsoever comes from a marriage based on a love charm. Hope I did the right thing.'

Love charm? Raven stared at the closed box. *Mr Odorless?* She must have misheard.

21. RECON AND INTEL

At some point Raven must have let slip to Morti about the secret den in Beechy Wood and that was it – Morti insisted this was the HQ they needed for solving Operation Pickles.

As Raven paced impatiently, waiting for Morti, she was pleased the table (or at least the slab of wood they had dragged halfway across Beechy Wood) was still there, as were the smaller trunks they'd lugged in to use for seats. It was smaller than she remembered and needed clearing out of dead leaves. But the

woodland xylophone remained. Rookery had meticulously put that together by hollowing branches of various sizes. So far it consisted of four notes. Was it too much to hope that Rookery might find time one day to come back and finish it?

Right now, Raven had a new panic. At the end of the school day, Mr Odorless had loomed over the Charming sisters as they walked towards the school gates: 'Rookery Charming – to my office, now!'

She'd helplessly watched her sister being silently led away. With all the strange happenings at the school, the teachers would be keeping an extra-vigilant eye on everything. Had Rookery let her magic slip again? Was it all over?

Raven had not been quick enough to find answers. After talking to Snapdragon and hearing that Mr Odorless of all people knew about magic she had become even more fearful that Rookery was only a step away from having to Deny Everything and right now her sister was in Mr Odorless's office, being grilled.

Morti had been quick to scramble off to listen at the door of the office, telling Raven he'd meet her in the den with intel as soon as he could. So Raven could do nothing except pace, hoping for more time to solve Operation Pickles. It couldn't all be down to Rookery, it couldn't. Mr Odorless couldn't have discovered Rookery was a witch. He couldn't have. Yet finding the right answers felt as far away as ever. Who had been mean enough to want to finish off Mr Pickles and leave him in the pond with his stuffing coming out? Not Rookery. Raven was sure.

The sound of rapid breathing told her Morti had run here all the way from school, although it might also be because he still thought the trees or the spiders might get him. He burst in, ducking under the branches that concealed the den from prying eyes. Raven took one look at his face, saw he was smiling and felt an enormous rush of relief.

'All OK! He's not accusing her of being a witch. He's accusing her of having sweets in school.'

Only a few days ago this would have been terrible news. Being caught with sweets by Mr Odorless was possibly more scary than being caught cheating in an exam. But now the important thing was that their time had not run out. They still had a chance to solve this puzzle and find out why the school was being cursed and how someone kept playing tricks without anyone seeing anything, and before anyone suspected it was Rookery. She really longed for Morti to instantly start planning his latest strat, but he seized a stick and went to tap out a tune on the woodland xylophone.

'Love our new HQ. You and Rookery really built all this?'

'We did think of building a proper tree house, on a platform up there.' Raven pointed.

'That would have been epic. Why didn't you?' said Morti.

'Well, the only way to do it was if Rookery moved all the wood with her mind.' And Raven could not have joined in.

'Being magic is so totally awesome, but what is it with you and magic? It's as if you don't really want it,' said Morti, sitting heavily on one of the squat tree-trunk seats. He extracted a packet of crushed prawn cocktail crisps, spreading them on the trunk table as if offering a feast. 'Help yourself.'

'It is difficult to truly imagine the difficulties,' said Nightshade, slipping down from a high branch. Raven hadn't even noticed her arrive.

'I'd rather have magic I had to keep a deadly secret rather than not have it at all,' said Morti through a mouthful of crisps. 'Could do with some magic on these crisps. It's only the crunch really makes them worthwhile and I haven't found a way of carrying them in my pocket without losing that.'

He swallowed and went back to fiddling with the makeshift xylophone. 'Now. Ready for recon and intel?'

'Yes!' breathed Raven. 'We need a next step for Operation Pickles.'

'Tertiary Phase,' corrected Morti. 'I've a feeling whoever is behind all this cursing and bad magic won't evade Operation Pickles for much longer.' Morti's eyes shone. 'Not now we've got this brilliant secret headquarters. We could do with a password. I'm working on it. And I have some exciting intel on Suspect Carsen.'

Raven looked at him eagerly. Morti was looking very pleased with himself. It was about time someone had intel that didn't point to Rookery.

'I don't think it's Carsen,' Morti said, before she had more than a second to hope.

Raven's heart sank.

'Carsen was dead shifty when I offered to help with Titus and I thought that was suspicious,' continued Morti, scoffing more crisps. 'You'd have thought he'd take all the help he could get braving that slobber. But Nightshade, you were dead right when you said everyone has a secret, but working out which ones are important is what makes you a good detective.'

'So I am guessing you have been a good detective and uncovered Carsen's secret?' said Nightshade, settling on a wide branch and tucking in her paws. 'I have been doing my bit and investigating Suspect Bianca, although mine has been a trickier assignment than it first appeared. I have made multiple visits in the name of thorough research.'

'Heh, heh, yeah yours is such a tough assignment. Don't suppose you manage to *investigate* Bianca by happening to go to the Maudlins' at teatime? I bet you're less stealth cat, more snooze cat after that salmon. Or fat cat. You wanna watch it.'

Nightshade silenced Morti with a hard stare from her green eyes.

'I have to drop in at that time,' she said, adopting a rather superior tone. 'I need to get there just before Mr Maudlin's home. He is a bit catist. And I've searched as much as I can. No sign of any magical artefacts, or books. No glittery green stone – I have been keeping my eyes peeled everywhere for that. I'm working up to getting into Bianca's room. Mrs Maudlin shoos me away. Reckons I'll leave hairs.'

'Well, the bad news is my crucial report on Secondary Phase doesn't get us any further either,' admitted Morti. 'So we knew Mr Odorless pays

Carsen to walk Titus. But the reason Carsen was shifty about me joining him isn't that he's worried I'll discover he's the Howling Hag's descendant and practising his magic on the school for some sort of evil revenge. You'll never guess what his secret is – he never actually walks that bit of carpet – 'cept that time I turned up and made him do it. He walks him as far as his home and hands him right over to his brother, who loves dogs. So it's Jackson who does the walking and he does it for nothing. Carsen just pockets Odorless's cash. That's a mean trick, right?'

'Sneaky,' agreed Nightshade. She pinged her claws. 'But not what we're looking for. Which is the same story at the Maudlins.'

She gave a snapshot of their dinner-time conversation: *Bianca: 'I'd really like a cat.' Mr Maudlin: 'No.' Bianca: 'Sian got a new pencil case today, it's beautiful and it's got a face on it.' Mr Maudlin: 'You had a new pencil case at the beginning of the year.' Bianca: 'Yes, but that's rank now, hardly fit to put my pencils in.' Mr Maudlin: 'It's just pencils, no.'*

'I don't believe it's getting us any further forward, but rest assured, I shall keep the Maudlins under surveillance.'

'As long as that salmon keeps arriving,' chuckled

Morti.

Nightshade pressed on. 'I have kept the house where Miss Percy and Miss Sunny live under surveillance too, as we are fast running through our prime suspects.'

'Miss Percy and Miss Sunny were nowhere near *Night Sky* when it fell,' pointed out Raven. 'Neither was Mr Odorless, unfortunately.'

Nightshade inclined her head. 'Miss Sunny is a cat lover all right, but Miss Percy is definitely more of a dog person and she tries to chase me out, so that has been a tricky assignment too, although I don't expect any thanks. The only window they leave open is on the first floor and it's inaccessible even for me, with my amazing agility. I think I may need to sneak in when they are out.'

Morti turned to Raven. 'Raven, shoot. Intel. All you have gathered from Primary and Secondary Phase. Go!'

Raven felt Nightshade's big green eyes focusing on her. 'I think you need to tell Morti *all* your news.'

From her pocket, she nervously took the scrap of burnt paper she had extracted from the embers of the fire. She flattened the singed remains out on to the table, brushing aside a couple of crisp crumbs and explaining where she had found it. Morti leant right in, his face contorting in a puzzled frown as he read the lettering out loud.

orld's Best Headte
ash i
mber Mr Pi

Then his face broke into a huge smile. 'Well, I know what this is!'

'Really? What is it?' asked Raven, puzzled.

'It's a clue. Isn't it?'

'Well, I thought it might be a spell, but it's not any sort of magic I can recognize,' sighed Raven. 'We've searched houses and haven't found a single shred of evidence that any of our suspects are involved in practising witchcraft.' She carried on in a small voice. 'Rookery has access to loads of spells.'

Morti looked closer and shook his head. 'It can't be a spell. Look – I think the first line's to do with head teacher – would you find that in a spell?' He pointed with a rather grubby finger. 'If it's a spell to make Mr Odorless the world's best head teacher, I have to say, it's not working.'

'I think you're right. But if it's not a spell, what would it be doing in the Howling Hag's fire? I've also discovered the inn was not named after a witch at all.' Raven passed on the news that until a few years ago it had been called something else entirely, avoiding confessing she'd got that information from Snapdragon. The mystery just seemed to be getting more baffling. Would they ever piece it all together?

Morti was digesting all Raven's news. 'You mean there's never been any other witch family in Twinhills? So the descendant idea isn't looking so hot? But it is magic? Otherwise, what's that fire behind the school for? And you found this in the fire?' He looked even more closely at the burnt scrap of paper.

Nightshade reminded him that all detectives could do was follow the evidence.

'If there's no revenge plot then we're a bit stuck for a motive for all these curses. I still say old Odorless is the only one with anything that even looks like a motive,' insisted Morti. 'There's no getting away from the fact that he'd go to any lengths to beat Fivetors at something.'

Raven recalled Morti muttering, '*Facts, motives, details, suspects, lies.*' What were they missing?

'I reckon Odorless spends more time on those sunflowers than he does in his office, since we lost that cricket match and time's running out to win anything,' Morti went on. 'And the curses are real.

Ella's shoes didn't move themselves. Sam must have been cursed to have lost at tennis and fumbled a catch the same week. And someone scissored Mr Pickles. So who's doing it? And how can someone pull off all this stuff, the theft, daubing the words on the wall, without anyone seeing anything? We were right in the hall when *Night Sky* crashed. You'd think being right there at the scene of the crime would give us some new clues.'

'Morti, you are right – it's a mystery,' Raven said, turning over everything in her mind and just wishing it would add up to an answer. 'I searched Rookery's room and there was no stone, money, nothing. So she's clear as a suspect,' she finished rapidly.

Nightshade shot her a look to remind her of her promise.

Morti groaned. 'We're running out of suspects and ideas. What do detectives do when they have run down every clue, exhausted every avenue and reached a dead end?'

'Have some more crisps?' suggested Raven.

Hearing Morti so deflated wasn't good, but Raven had promised Nightshade to come clean about everything and she had one more thing to share. She pressed on, confessing about the mask she had found in Rookery's room.

'I don't know what it means, I don't know if it's even connected.'

Morti scraped the last of the crisps into his mouth. 'Like Nightshade says, all we can do is look at the evidence.' He suddenly looked more cheerful 'Oh, I get it! I get what you're saying. If we follow the evidence, there is only one conclusion, isn't there? You're saying your sister is now pretty much Number One suspect.'

22. WHAT SORT OF NASTY ACCIDENT?

Raven leapt to her feet. 'Rookery wouldn't deliberately do anything bad. She would never have stolen that money or killed Mr Pickles. What I'm saying is that things are even more complicated, and darker, than we thought.'

'Well, I just love it when we reach the really impenetrable part of a mystery,' said Nightshade, cheerfully pinging a claw again. 'And I don't think we've exhausted every lead.'

'Of course! I completely forgot I have a plan for

searching Aaliyah's sheep bag. Told you I'd work on Operation Pickles, Secondary Phase, Extension Mode.' Morti's eyes glinted as he looked at Raven. 'I think you are going to have a nasty accident.'

'What!'

'We need a clue that doesn't point to your sister. We need more intel. All you need to do is get yourself an injury, say you need to go and get plasters from Bianca's mum.' Morti went on thoughtfully, 'Do it in PE.'

'Surprised there are any plasters left the way the Miss Percy's class have taken to wearing them,' muttered Nightshade. 'Your school is like one infectious plastery rash.'

'I'm not sure I really want an injury,' said Raven, sitting down again.

Morti rolled his eyes. 'Not a real one, otherwise that defeats the whole strat. You're not really going to get a plaster. Just splatter some red sauce around. Make it look good enough to deceive the untrained eye. Wouldn't fool us detectives, of course. I'll nab some extra sauce in lunch.'

'But—?'

'Well, what other excuse are you going to give to sneak out of PE and into the girls' cloakroom to have a delve in Aaliyah's bag? We need to see what Aaliyah's hiding in that sheep bag. Or had you forgotten? Told you she started out being the least likely suspect, probably means it's her all along.'

Raven's tree-trunk seat was starting to feel hard and uncomfortable. She was beginning to have so many doubts they were feeling like a cloud about to rain inside her head. She was glad that Morti could stay focused. He was right to remind her that she suspected Aaliyah knew something. She had to cling on to the fact that there had to be an answer and a way out of this mess that wasn't going to lead to dropping her sister in it.

'I'm dead jealous,' said Morti. 'Not about you sneaking into the girls' cloakroom obviously, which is why this mission has to be you. But you get another chance to go covert.'

Nightshade swished her tail. 'Talking of searching, your Rookery getting dragged off to Mr Odorless's office reminded me – he's always confiscating sweets, isn't he? We all agree that if we could find the glittery stone stolen from Miss Percy's locked box it would help to point us in the right direction? Well, he keeps everything he's confiscated in a big trunk under his desk in his office.' She licked a paw. 'Wonder if he stashed the stone in there?'

'Sherlock Holmes cat! How d'you even know about the trunk?' demanded Morti.

'I keep my whiskers to the ground. I'd love to do the actual searching, of course, but don't point your paws at me.' Nightshade padded down from her branch. 'What if there's a fiddly catch? No chance with soft paws like mine. And my lack of opposable thumbs. One of the advantages humans do have over cats, although you are lousy at climbing trees. One of you two needs to slip in and open that trunk. I would suggest doing it while the other creates a distraction.'

Neg woke up inside Raven and her stomach wobbled like jelly at even the thought of stepping into Odorless's office.

'Right!' said Morti. 'Let's draw for who searches Odorless's office. I'd call heads or tails, but I don't have any coins. We could rock, paper, scissors it? Or –' he fished around and produced a small white bag from which he extracted a long and lurid red sweet – 'they call 'em jelly slugs at your village shop, but I call 'em jelly worms. Worms is better, I reckon.'

'I don't think it makes all that much difference,' said Raven, staring at the brightly coloured sweet.

Morti put his hands behind his back and then presented two closed fists to Raven to choose between. 'If you guess the hand with the slug in it, you go covert and break into the trunk.'

If she got the slug, she would be brave. *This was for Rookery*, Raven told herself. She looked at Morti's closed fists. It was impossible to tell which contained the slug. His face gave nothing away.

She tapped his right fist and he turned it over and uncurled his fingers revealing the stickiness of a red jelly slug kept in a warm hand just too long.

Raven's heart thundered as Morti transferred it to her hand, but she nodded, trying to find a face that would look a lot braver than she felt.

'Nightshade and I will work on a diversion,' Morti said. 'Reckon we can give you ten minutes, easy. The rest is up to you.'

Raven looked at the jelly slug, its stickiness starting to ooze.

'Oh, that's yours,' Morti added generously. 'You can eat it if you want to.'

23. Too Many Kittens

I slipped through the wrought-iron railings and padded along the Maudlins' immaculate lawn, soft as a carpet on my paws, hurrying to make it before the daily offering of salmon was whisked away. Mrs Maudlin could be a little pernickety about leaving fish around in the hot weather. I appreciated the concern. Such a thoughtful person, Mrs Maudlin. A family very keen on their pets.

I was looking forward as much to the fish as to that silk cushion placed right in a sunny patch, ready

for a little nap afterwards. I'd heard how Mrs Maudlin once found homes for seven unexpected kittens, and that put her high on my list of favourite people in Twinhills.

Mr Maudlin was a different matter.

After a day at work, his way of relaxing was to silently frown at a really thick book at the dinner table. There was never a lot of chat. I wasn't finding out anything interesting. But my plan was to listen to Mrs Maudlin as well as Bianca. It wasn't easy to imagine either risking breaking into anything to help themselves to someone else's money – but Mrs M worked in school gossip central: the office. If there was one person who would know what the teachers suspected about the unexplained things disappearing and appearing, it was kitten-loving Mrs Maudlin. So I listened up and hoped for intel.

'Can you believe Rookery doesn't have any pets?' Bianca said, buttering a roll thickly. 'I said to get a hamster, then she could bring it here and they could play together. Or I could get another. But Rookery said hamsters fight. She knows so much for someone who doesn't have one. So maybe a guinea pig.'

I gave a little miaow to Mrs Maudlin. She understood, without all the effort with the eyes. *I'm thirsty today and require a top-up of milk, please.* The

Maudlins were having a very big cream cake for pudding. I could hope for a slice; I could hope the conversation would switch to something interesting. But I expected the usual: just crumbs.

'Why are we feeding a darn stray cat?' Mr Maudlin had stuck his thumb in his pages to keep his place and his eyes were not fixed on his grim book of war stories, but on me. And in a distinctly unfriendly fashion. 'I expressly forbade cats in the house. I hope you have not forgotten what happened last time.'

Stray! But at least the conversation seemed to have taken an unexpected turn.

I put on my best beseeching big eyes and did the usual. I purred like a steam train rattling along a country track, a sound I have perfected over several years. A purr practically guaranteed to have the desired winning-over effect.

'It's just eaten a bigger piece of fish than me. Have you any idea how much salmon costs?'

My detective senses were telling me that maybe Mrs M whisked away that salmon so quickly not for fear of food poisoning in this warm weather, but to remove the evidence before her husband came home.

I went and rubbed around his legs, still purring.

'And now it's putting hair all over my trousers!'

Mr Maudlin moved his legs sharply. Almost enough to be called a kick.

Time for a dignified retreat. A change of strategy was required.

I dived through the tangle of human feet and table legs and squeezed myself on to Bianca's lap. He may not want to buy his daughter a new pencil case every time she feared her pencils were getting dirty, but there wasn't much Mr Maudlin wouldn't do for her.

'Snoozy really does like us the best,' she said, delightedly fussing my ears. She was a lovely girl and I was almost getting used to being called Snoozy. 'Although Raven says she's called Nightshade.'

Mr Maudlin went back to his book, but didn't turn any pages for a while. It was a serious book full of long words and difficult thoughts, but maybe he was just waiting for what Bianca was going to ask for next.

'Nightshade is not really mine.' Sigh. 'I'd love a kitten.'

'We are not getting a kitten,' said Mrs M gently. 'Your father is firm about that.'

'Guinea pigs then. They don't fight. If you have more than one.'

'And what about your new hamster? We've only

just got Gerald,' spoke up Mr Maudlin, without looking up from brooding over his challenging pages.

'Lady McFluff,' corrected Bianca. 'Or maybe two birds. They could sing to each other.'

I pricked up my ears at the idea of a bird. A bird sounded better than that hamster. All day locked in a cage and only let out to run around in a big plastic ball, which is a lot less fun than it sounds.

Mr Maudlin peered at his wife. 'We did have a bird and you loved that thing. Sang. I don't remember it being a lot of trouble.'

Mrs M was busying herself with clearing the table. 'Not a bird.'

'Better than those awful hairy rabbits!'

'I loved those rabbits,' said Bianca. 'Rookery says their noses are waffly.'

'Ah no, now I remember about that bird. Little Miss Tweets was trouble,' said Mr Maudlin. 'Lost her voice after some bird flu and the vet said there was nothing that could be done – and as for what happened next!'

Mrs M dropped a heavy spoon on to a plate with a crash that hurt my ears.

'You called on that woman. Used to teach yoga in the village hall. Everyone whispered about her,' went on Mr Maudlin. 'What was her name?'

'Whispered?' said Bianca curiously. She was quite forgetting to stroke my ears. She hadn't even asked for pudding. 'What did they whisper?'

'Oh, you know, the kind of superstitious nonsense you get in Twinhills. Someone gives you funny-coloured lemonade to drink and says a couple of strange words and tells you it's a miracle cure. Your mother fell for all that nonsense.'

Bianca looked with wide-open eyes at her dad. 'Mum went to a witch?' She looked at both her parents. 'You never told me we have an actual witch living in Twinhills. You never tell me anything interesting.'

There was an uncomfortable silence.

'I'd like curly hair like Raven Charming,' went on Bianca, looking thoughtful. 'Her hair looks so soft it makes you want to ask if you can touch it. I could ask a witch.'

Mrs M got very busy stacking plates. 'I don't believe she did actual *spells*. She was good with healings and cures and giving good luck, I'll give her that. Anyway, she didn't like the name "witch". Preferred being called *enchantress*.'

'Didn't stop you consulting her,' said Mr Maudlin.

Mrs M took the plates into the kitchen and

Bianca got up to follow a little hurriedly, tipping me to the floor.

'Do you know that people get witches all wrong?' Bianca said eagerly. 'A lot of what we think is the history about them is just not true. Witches were OK until Henry the Eighth made them illegal. Lots of countries had a witch-hunting craze and killed loads. Burning at the stake wasn't common everywhere. Most used to hang them if they were found guilty.'

I had a nasty feeling Rookery had been over-sharing with her best friend.

'Thank you. What a delightful subject,' said Mr Maudlin. 'If only you put as much effort into your studies as your sudden interest in witchcraft and your obsession with pets.'

Mrs M stalked past Bianca and placed pudding dishes on the table.

'Did the witch cure Little Miss Tweets with her magic?' Bianca demanded the end of the story.

Mr Maudlin said: 'Yes, you tell her. You went to that Charming woman with that terrible witchy name – Snapdragon, wasn't it? You thought magic would somehow help when everyone else had given up on your precious bird. And did the witch let you down at all, dear?'

'That Charming woman?' Bianca's eyes opened wide. 'The person who tried to cure Little Miss Tweets was . . . Oh, please tell me what happened.'

Mrs Maudlin shook a little salt into her hand, grabbed a piece of leftover bread from the table, dabbed it in the salt and threw it over her shoulder.

'What on earth are you doing?' asked Bianca, staring.

'Cross a piece of bread with salt. Avoid a witch's evil clutches,' said Mrs Maudlin in a very low voice and with an anxious glance at her husband.

The last thing I'd been expecting was a lesson in witch lore from Mrs Maudlin. Dodgy witch lore mind you, but still.

'I went to her for a consultation, then she completely vanished,' said Mrs Maudlin sadly, cutting a thick wedge of cream cake. Not for me, I guessed.

Bianca's eyes went almost round with surprise and then narrowed with suspicion. 'Something bad happened? Do you think witchcraft is behind all the bad stuff happening at school?'

Mrs Maudlin silently handed Bianca the thick wedge of cake and poured on a dollop of extra cream. I licked my lips.

'Come on, Mum. Money stolen and no one able

to explain it. Mr Pickles, stabbed. Pictures falling off walls. Something's at work. Something powerful. I think it'll take more than a pinch of salt and a bit of dry bread to cure Twinhills of witches being at work.'

'What's this nonsense?' spluttered Mr Maudlin.

Mrs M headed to the kitchen and Bianca went and leant against the door.

'So you consulted a witch and Little Miss Tweets never sang again? I bet that made you sad.'

Mrs M scraped plates noisily, but I was listening hard to every word. 'Now I know you are best friends with Rookery and she seems like a nice girl –' I only just caught the last words of advice Mrs Maudlin said under her breath to her daughter – 'but be warned, you must have nothing to do with witches, Bianca.'

24. THE EXPLODING LUNCH BAG

Miss Percy and Miss Sunny's classes had been told to get changed for PE early and then gather together outside for a treat to make up for missing out on their survival lesson. Miss Percy was going to do a science experiment.

'If she's doing it outside it means it's going to be noisy and smelly,' Raven told Morti, his eyes lighting up as they joined in the jostling for the best view.

'If the worst happens and it goes wrong there might be injuries. We might get a day off school,' he said.

Everyone craned their necks as Miss Percy showed them a large clear plastic bag, a sheet of kitchen paper and a thermos flask.

'Sure she's doing science? Looks more like we've all followed her to where she planned to be alone to eat extra lunch,' joked Carsen.

'Perhaps she needs the energy boost before cricket training,' said Sam.

Miss Percy lifted the thermos. 'In this I have vinegar, warmed. I will put bicarbonate of soda on this kitchen paper. Together, they will make – an explosion.'

This brought more than a frisson of excited chatter.

'So I need everyone to stand well back,' said Miss Percy as everyone lurched forward. 'This is going to get messy.'

It didn't take long for Raven to hear the whispers. *Where's the Howling Hag?*

'Just ready for the Howling Hag to do something mad, aren't they?' grinned Morti.

'How did that even start?' muttered Raven to herself, watching the faces of all her school friends, all eagerly focusing on Miss Percy, longing for the promised explosion, but also looking about, not knowing where the next piece of malice would come from.

Everyone else was enthralled, but Raven was distracted – still looking for any explanation for the curses that didn't involve her very magical sister. Why would anyone want to curse the school? Was it possible that the Howling Hag was right here, now, among them, about to strike again?

She knew she had taken too long to recognize that something sinister was going on. Even when the words *Watch out! I am here and I am going to eat you* had appeared, written large on Miss Sunny's board, she'd dismissed them as a joke. How many unsettling things had happened before people started to think they were linked? When had the fear and the chanting begun?

She had been slow to notice also because occasionally her sister *did* do magic at school. Unusual things *did* happen at Twinhills. When had things become cruel? She had been going over everything. Nightshade had been doing exactly the same – the black cat had caught up with her on the way into school with another piece of evidence – something else that didn't add up and only made things more confused. They were both desperate to work out how the magic was being done. It felt good to have the cat watching over her.

With everyone so focused on Miss Percy it was

easy for Raven's mind to wander. She thought about Ella being a hero for scoring the impossible winning goal in football.

That had been down to Rookery, Raven was sure. Henry Figgins squirting himself with pink paint after ruining Rookery's picture – sadly that had been her sister too. Not Rookery's kindest moment, true. But Raven was sure she must have spent a long time untangling Everly's kite, only to secretly leave it on her desk, never receiving any thanks. That was exactly the sort of kind thing Rookery would do with her magic.

Ella's fancy shoes being pinched and humiliatingly displayed on the spelling trophy would not be Rookery. She had no quarrel with teeny-tiny chattery Ella. Sam had burnt his hand and lost a tennis match and fumbled that critical catch in a game with Fivetors in a disastrous week. Morti was convinced that had to be a curse. The theft of the money and the stone had stepped things up, made it look like the Howling Hag could do anything, was powerful enough to get away with anything.

Then things had got dangerous with the death of Mr Pickles. The Howling Hag's hold over Twinhills was growing, yet Snapdragon had been adamant there was no such person, it was just a story. Like what Morti thought he knew about witches – that all came from stories.

'I'm going to pour this warmed vinegar into this plastic bag,' Miss Percy was carrying on. 'Then I'm going to wrap the bicarbonate of soda in kitchen paper and drop it in. A reaction will occur in the plastic bag, causing it to expand with gas. Can anyone tell me what gas?'

Henry Figgins' hand went right up. 'Carbon dioxide, miss.' He went into an explanation about acids and how the gas would make bubbles and they could watch the bag expanding until it eventually exploded.

'Excellent chemistry, Henry,' said Miss Percy.

The questions kept churning around Raven's mind. Why would someone curse the school? Was there any sort of pattern to what was happening? When Miss Percy had failed to open the padlock, stopping them getting into Beechy Wood for their survival lesson, the whispering and the chanting had started up immediately. Raven hadn't been able to detect any signs of anyone doing magic. The message Nightshade had delivered that morning was that she'd inspected that lock and found it had been stuffed with glue.

Miss Percy carried on. 'I'll have to work fast once

I've dropped it in.' Everyone crowded a little closer and Miss Percy again asked them to stay back.

'Morti, do your parents move around mostly because you are always in trouble and getting thrown out of schools?'

Morti shifted uncomfortably. 'Nah, it's just Mum and Dad's work.'

When she first heard that the Scratches moved around because he was trouble it had made her nervous of him. But now she knew him, she guessed that was just a story. How easy it was to start a rumour.

'I probably shouldn't have tapped Henry on the nose for making fun of me my first day. It was a bit harsh,' he shrugged. 'But the last school I was at you had to stand up for yourself. Twinhills is much nicer. I'd like to stay.'

'You'd like to stay at a cursed school, even with the Howling Hag?'

'Well, we're sorting that out, aren't we? You should do it now, you know,' said Morti, giving Raven a nudge with his elbow. 'Don't wait for PE, everyone's eyes on are on this. Go search Aaliyah's bag. No one's going to notice.'

Morti was right. But Raven hesitated. She wasn't ready. Would she be any more ready during PE?

Then there was a familiar sound. Mr Odorless's door opened and he scuttled on his short legs across the playground, in such a hurry that today he hadn't even lingered to grab his coffee to bring with him.

Miss Percy watched the head's approach. 'Ah, Mr Odorless. Nice of you to join us.'

'I am curious. What is happening?' he asked, putting his head on one side and speaking in a way that said he had come to put a stop to this as it looked like it might be fun.

'I thought that as we failed to get to our outdoors lesson in Beechy Wood this week, I would treat the children to an entertaining experiment,' said Miss Percy, maintaining a bright tone and fixed smile.

'Go now,' said Morti out of the side of his mouth. 'Now Odorless is here. You could kill two birds with one stone and search his office. I'll tell Miss Percy you've gone for plasters. I got your mission kit.' He slid her a sachet of red sauce from his pocket.

Mr Odorless looked around at the eagerly watching children. 'Ah well, fun and treats are what we are here for, aren't they? Such a shame you were unable to get to the wood this week. Although it did give us the chance to do spelling. Perhaps we can—'

'It was the Howling Hag,' said Aaliyah simply.

'She doesn't want us in the wood. And if we upset her she'll bake us in an oven and eat us.'

Mr Odorless moved in close to Aaliyah. His face was turning purple. 'We do not talk nonsense like that in this school, not ever! Or you will have to come to my office and explain why.'

Aaliyah, already tiny, appeared to visibly shrink.

'But what about Gregor Tomkins?' came a voice from the back – Sam Carruthers. 'Didn't he get eaten? That's what I heard.'

Mr Odorless scoured the throng with his beady eyes, looking for the voice that dared question him. 'Eaten? Gregor Tomkins? Nonsense! His family moved away.'

'Ah,' said Sam. 'I thought the Howling Hag got him like she did Mr Pickles.' He mimed getting scissors in his stomach to some general murmurs of agreement.

Mr Odorless said very slowly and quietly, with one of his awful smiles: 'You all want a lesson outside? We could all go and weed the sunflowers? Or did I hear someone say you wanted a little test right here?'

And Mr Odorless began to fire spellings at them like bullets. 'Conscientious, minuscule, grotesque, banister – someone tell me if that has got one "n" or two.' All the worst and trickiest words that no one, not even the good spellers, could ever put in a sentence. 'We were working on words beginning with C last time. How about *culpable*? Maybe it's Miss Percy who needs to learn how to put that in a sentence.'

Raven didn't wait to hear Mr Odorless give his dry chuckle which sounded like leaves being crushed. She successfully shuffled backwards away from the crowd. Even the utterly rubbish seeing crystal could predict what was likely to happen if she got caught breaking into Mr Odorless's office, and her heart was hammering as she slipped away.

But the stolen stone was one of their last leads. If they were going to expose who was behind the bad luck and curses, she had to find it.

25. STAYING ONE STEP AHEAD OF MR ODORLESS

Everyone was either glued to watching for the moment Miss Percy set off the explosion, or looking fearfully at the head teacher. Raven slipped away.

Morti was right. Mr Odorless had rushed out of his office so quickly he'd even left behind his coffee – and he had left the door open. Now was her chance, because she felt Mr Odorless was the most likely to be the Howling Hag, it was just that they could find no evidence to prove it. So far.

It was the answer that made most sense. Morti

had said all Mr Odorless really cared about was beating Fivetors at something, and he was certainly not above using fear or magic, or anything that would improve their chances.

Raven had never been inside Mr Odorless's office before. She wasn't surprised that it was exceedingly neat, with a big noticeboard full of sticky reminders, books arranged according to height and a desk clear except for piles of pages of extra-boring homework ideas and seriously tough maths equations, plus paper that looked ready for writing out lines. And his World's Best Head Teacher mug with a slop of coffee still in the bottom. The whole room smelt of milky coffee and recent hoovering.

Where was this trunk? Nightshade had said under the desk. Raven moved aside the big comfy swivel chair, and noticed a file marked *Top Secret and Urgent* sitting on it. Raven reached out one nervous finger to see if she could sneak a look inside. She felt she was being watched by all the pictures on the noticeboard behind the desk: Mr Odorless posing proudly and beaming with various happy-looking parents. His biggest smile was at the ceremony for last year's attempt to grow the tallest sunflowers. Twinhills had lost out by five centimetres. She twitched open the lid on the secret file . . . and discovered a stash of extra-crunchy biscuits.

Raven ducked under the desk. Nightshade was exactly right about the big trunk. Raven kneeled to examine it – if it was locked or padlocked she'd be sunk. Last night, she'd even practised an unlocking charm sneaked from one of Mum's books, even though there was little point. *As if you could get magic to work*, she heard Neg whisper.

Outside, she could hear Mr Odorless firing spelling orders at everyone.

'Convenience. We don't seem to be running out of Cs. Confluence.'

She felt safe for the moment, and doubly lucky when the trunk wasn't locked. But the lid was heavy and she was struggling to lift it.

Then, from her kneeling position, she saw the door open.

Raven froze, hoping being crouched under the desk would be enough not to be seen. But how was she going to get out? She was trapped. Who was it?

She had a clear view and was amazed that walking softly through the door, sneaking a hasty, nervous glance over his shoulder, was Sam Carruthers. Had he come to search the trunk for something Mr Odorless had confiscated? If so, Raven was sunk.

Sam approached the desk, and before Raven

could even begin to hope she was small and crouched enough to not be seen, he said: 'Hello Raven, what are you doing?'

'Well, what are you doing, Sam?' asked Raven, feeling her face burning as she focused on getting up – it was difficult to look brave when you were cowering under a desk.

'Are you here on a mission for the Howling Hag?' he asked.

'Mission for the Howling Hag? I'm just trying to get something from Mr Odorless's trunk,' said Raven. 'But the lid's heavy.'

'Sure, got it.' Sam gave her a conspiratorial wink and pushed his floppy blond hair out of his eyes. He came to help and together they managed to lift the lid in the cramped space under the desk. Raven stared at the impressive stash of sweets and biscuits.

How on earth was she going to find a sparkly green stone in all this?

She began to rummage. Even Mr Odorless couldn't keep firing spellings for ever. 'Sam, you couldn't help me, could you?'

Sam had grabbed Mr Odorless's World's Best Head Teacher mug from the desk. It was still half full of coffee. 'No, I just came for this.' He was already heading for the door.

Raven stared at the mug, completely flummoxed. 'Why d'you want that?'

He shrugged nonchalantly, as if sneaking into Mr Odorless's office was just normal for him, whereas Raven was beginning to tremble like a leaf as she tried to work her way through confiscated crisps, biscuits, sweets, a catapult, a game of marbles and a rather offensive joke book. She could not find that stone.

'My turn. Again.'

'Turn?' Raven watched, utterly bewildered, as he tipped the slops of coffee into a handy rubber plant. 'You've broken into Mr Odorless's office before?' Raven stopped rummaging through all the illicit goodies.

'No,' he said, as if she was being slow. 'The Howling Hag. Well, you have to, don't you?' He shrugged, as if this explained everything.

Raven could only splutter: 'The Howling Hag! You mean . . . you're the one doing all the disappearing tricks and curses? It's you?' Her eyes widened. Was he admitting it? She felt cross that Sam had never made it on to their list of top suspects even with all their careful detecting. She waited – she had a feeling that wasn't what he was saying at all. But what was he saying?

Sam grinned. 'Ah, then you don't know.' He

winked. 'That's not how it works.'

'How does it work?

'You'll find out when you move up to Miss Percy's class. Thought I was going to fail this time. Couldn't believe my luck when I saw him striding out to have a go at Miss Percy and finally let go of this mug. My lucky day Miss Percy decided to do an explosion. Thought he was going to explode when I got cursed last time and lost to Fivetors at cricket.'

Sam pointed to the photos on the noticeboard behind the desk. 'He really has a thing about beating them, doesn't he?'

Raven looked at the photos again. Several were newspaper cuttings featuring the same serious-looking woman. Raven recognized her. The cuttings were about the amazing achievements of Fivetors. The woman was the head of Fivetors, Miss Earnest.

The most enormous *POP!* from outside signalled the explosive end of Miss Percy's science experiment.

'Sam, please can you help me?'

He looked towards the door and freedom and then back at Raven. 'What did you say you were doing?'

Raven resumed rummaging frantically through the trunk. 'I'm looking for the sparkly green stone that disappeared, as if by magic, from the locked box in Miss Percy's desk.'

'Why on earth do you want that? I don't think it's going to be here.'

The way he said that told Raven he knew something. 'Why do you say that, Sam?'

But Sam only answered by giving a lopsided grin, but came back to help her reach right to the bottom. There was no stone. Raven was so disappointed not to have found the evidence they were searching for. She looked again at Sam, suspecting he knew something about the Hag. She just wished she had a clue what it was, or how to get him to share what he knew.

But Sam escaped to freedom clutching the stolen mug, and Raven noticed something else she should have spotted right away. On the fingers clutching Mr Odorless's World's Best Head Teacher mug were plasters.

Raven scrambled to her feet to catch Sam before she lost her chance.

'Sam. Your fingers . . . you haven't burnt them again? Do the burnt fingers mean something? Sam, do you know who the Howling Hag really is?'

'Wouldn't we all like to know that! Don't tell anyone that I swiped this.' He raised the mug like a trophy. 'Remember what happened to Mr Pickles.' And then he was gone.

26. Mournful Sheep

She had just caught Sam doing . . . well, she had
caught him doing something, she wasn't exactly
sure what. Swiping Mr Odorless's precious mug.
And hadn't he said this wasn't his first turn doing
something? When she'd asked if he'd done all the
curses, he'd replied, *That's not how it works.*

What did that mean? And hadn't Aaliyah used
almost exactly the same words?

Aaliyah. From the noises outside it was easy to tell
Raven had missed the start of PE. Raven's part in

going covert for Operation Pickles was not yet over. PE was when she'd planned to sneak a look into the secrets contained in the mournful sheep bag. So instead of heading outside for catching practice, she headed swiftly to the girls' changing room.

Nightshade had insisted they follow the evidence, and that trail now led her to the mournful sheep bag hanging on a peg. She stared at it, breathing a little quickly and feeling as if they were as far as ever from solving the mystery of the Howling Hag.

When Nightshade had mentioned her idea about the trunk, she'd been so pleased that Mr Odorless was back in the running for being the Howling Hag. It was disappointing to have failed to find that green stone – they needed solid evidence.

Raven was turning over everything in her mind as she fumbled to unfasten the bag. Aaliyah knew something, she was sure. But so did Sam. And so, for that matter, did Rookery.

Simply touching the sheep bag made Raven feel afraid, as if something was warning her, giving her a feeling of smoke and fire – her fingers throbbed and she almost dropped it.

She recalled the nervous way Aaliyah had kept touching it with her injured fingers, while denying she had stolen the stone and the twenty pounds, even though Raven hadn't even asked her. Aaliyah was surely way too timid to be the daring Howling Hag, despite Morti's insistence that she had to be a strong suspect exactly because she was the least likely person. But could they get Aaliyah to talk.

When she peeped inside she could hardly believe what she was staring at, not believing the evidence of her own eyes. There was the pretty green stone with the hole they had searched everywhere for, just sitting there. But also twenty pounds that surely had to be the money swiped from Miss Percy's desk.

Raven found she couldn't move, even though she knew she had to go. Should she seize this evidence? Would Morti and Nightshade believe her? Because they'd all agreed whoever had stolen the stone had to be the Howling Hag.

Aaliyah had the stone.

Then Aaliyah had to be the Howling Hag. *Aaliyah?*

PART FOUR

27. Killing a Witch is Not Easy

All the way home Raven asked herself the seriously big question. Was timid, always-follow-the-rules Aaliyah the one putting a curse on the school?

Even seeing the evidence, the conclusion felt wrong and she needed to talk to someone, someone who knew about magic. She arrived home, determined to talk to Rookery, but she'd forgotten it was Photography Club day. Rookery would be home late.

Raven's own guilty secret was hidden in the bottom

of her wardrobe. After talking to Snapdragon, she'd brought the music box home with her.

She didn't know how the precious box had ended up behind all those jams at the back of a kitchen cupboard, even in the untidiness of Dandelion Cottage. It was easy to picture Knox putting it there when he'd meant to put it somewhere else entirely. But she didn't know how long she could risk holding on to it without Knox missing it.

She carried it carefully past Mum, who was busy at her desk, and right to the bottom of the garden where a gate opened out on to one of the many footpaths that criss-crossed Twinhills. She sat under the shade of the apple tree (luckily the metal was all back in the house), suddenly missing Dad. The garden should be full of digging, planting and pruning to make things beautiful. Sadly his conference on building roads with fewer holes had been struck by ironic misfortune when a giant sinkhole had appeared outside the conference centre and trapped everyone. Dad could see the funny side of not being able to leave. It sounded as if he was the only one who could.

As Raven took out the box it felt warm and alive. She gently turned the winder. She could only hope she wasn't endangering Snapdragon by waking her again, but Raven felt only her grandma could possibly help.

As the tinkly version of 'Danse Macabre' began, Raven considered how you often found out things by listening when you shouldn't, particularly when adults are talking in low voices and you can look really busy with a jigsaw puzzle, because they think that makes your ears stop working.

That's how she had learnt all she knew about Snapdragon's accident while collecting ingredients, how her brown satchel had been found at the bottom of the hanging tree, surrounded by smashed bottles of unnamed spells. She'd overheard Knox saying in a hushed voice that no one was sure if Snapdragon had been involved in an accident, or possibly attacked. That was why Raven had gone very quiet when Morti went on about how the hanging tree could have a connection to villagers disposing of their unwanted witches.

Since discovering the secret of the music box, she'd wondered if Mum and Knox had decided it was safer for Snapdragon to remain hidden. It all felt like another thing that you never got a straight answer about in their family. Raven certainly wasn't going to confess that she'd first opened the box by accident and had now woken Snapdragon a couple of times. As she held the box gently, she couldn't help but feel a panic at the thought she might be harming her grandma by waking her.

But it was too late to worry. The black triangles on the top began to twitch and move outwards to create the dark hollow in the centre.

'Grandma, is there some sort of magic that controls people and gets them to do things against their will?' Raven asked quickly, as soon as Snapdragon got out of her tree pose and blinked at her without her glasses.

'Don't call me Grandma, there's a dear. I am Antirrhinum Wilhelmina Charming, but everyone calls me Snapdragon.'

This was bad – Snapdragon didn't seem to be as awake as usual and didn't even appear to recognize Raven. Raven felt even more guilty for waking her so soon after last time. But as she debated if she should just close the lid, Snapdragon seemed to perk up and stretched into another yoga pose.

'Mind control spells? You'd be surprised what some truly powerful magicians can do. It's not for you to do yourself, is it, lovely Raven? Slipping into the sinister side of magic? That's not where your path or your powers lie. But if you think someone else is doing it, you might want to know how to spot it and how to stop it, I guess.'

Raven breathed out a 'Yes!' Snapdragon always managed to listen and understand what Raven was trying to say.

'It would be seriously impressive magic,' said Snapdragon. 'You asked me about another witch in Twinhills.'

Raven was glad she'd remembered. 'I did. It is difficult to identify a witch, isn't it? And to know for sure if magic is being done.'

'Of course. But trust your senses, dear Raven.'

'Could Rookery do that magic – the mind control?'

'Oh goodness me.' Snapdragon sounded all fluttery.

This was the thought that kept nudging at Raven like a loose tooth. She'd tried to make sense of that conversation with Sam, then tried to remember exactly what Aaliyah had said. She had put back the stone and the money in the mournful sheep bag and tried to get it all to add up.

Then, at the end of PE, Mr Odorless's World's Best Head Teacher mug had been discovered smashed to pieces in front of Miss Percy's classroom. The chanting had begun. *The Howling Hag!* Everyone leapt straight to the conclusion that this was more magic, another curse. The mug had moved by itself! But Raven had seen the mug move. And Sam.

And it was not magic that had spirited that mug out of Mr Odorless's office. It had been Sam Carruthers, slipping in when everyone was focused on something else. Obey-the-rules Aaliyah had never taken that money to spend it; she'd just kept it in her bag. So why take it at all?

That's not how it works, both of them had said. Sam had also said about it being his turn again, and not to tell but to remember Mr Pickles. Both of them had hurt their fingers. Carsen too. What was that all about?

Raven hadn't had a chance to report back to Morti and Nightshade yet. She made her brain hurt wondering: were any of the curses magic at all?

Snapdragon adopted another uncomfortable yoga pose as Raven sat in the shade of the apple tree at the bottom of the garden, thinking and waiting. Snapdragon was still considering her question about Rookery's powers.

They assumed the stone and the money must have been taken by magic, because it would have taken so much time to find the key to unlock the box and no one had seen anything – particularly Aaliyah, who had been in the classroom the entire time. Everyone had whispered the chant and everyone just said it was the Howling Hag again and Raven had never properly considered the most simple explanation – Aaliyah had plenty of chance to unlock the box. Aaliyah had taken the money and the stone.

But Aaliyah hadn't done *all* the curses. Because Sam had stolen Mr Odorless's mug and presumably smashed it. And everyone had said that was magic.

Who was the Howling Hag? Aaliyah? Sam? Was Mr Odorless still the best suspect? Or Rookery – she couldn't rule her out.

Maybe if different people were behind each curse and no one saw, no one talked about it . . . someone still had to be behind it. That's when she'd hit on the theory. Maybe it was some kind of mind-control magic. What if someone was making people do things?

Snapdragon was silent and thoughtful long enough for Raven to dread the answer. How powerful was her sister? Why would Rookery want everyone in the school terrified and being controlled?

'No one knows how powerful a witch your sister might be one day.' Snapdragon appeared to be fully awake now. 'But she's a beginner – so far she can only really do one kind of magic. It would take a powerful sorcerer but also experience to do any kind of mind-control spell.'

Raven waited for the rush of relief, but could only really, really hope Snapdragon was right. Even if she was, that still left the big question. Were they up against someone very magical indeed in Twinhills?

'You started to say something before about my head teacher,' said Raven. 'He consulted you about a spell? I wondered if you were trying to warn me that he's a powerful sorcerer.'

'Tony Odorless? A sorcerer? No, dear.'

'But he knows about magic?'

'Well, yes, but not sinister magic and mind control. He wanted a love potion, dearie – you have no idea how often I get asked for those.'

There was the noise of passing footsteps in the lane that ran along the bottom of the garden, but there was no way Raven was stopping. She dropped her voice. 'Mr Odorless wanted a love potion?'

'I thought afterwards the poor dear probably only wanted it to give him some confidence, bless him. I upset him when I refused, I know. But really – is that going to lead to a happy marriage – someone who has been tricked into it by magic? That's the question I always ask myself. I try only to do good with my magic.'

Raven could not even begin to process this information.

'It's always disappointing when you let someone down,' went on Snapdragon. 'But what would the world be if everyone thought all their problems should be fixed by casting a spell rather than working things through for themselves? It's one of the reasons it is so important magic remains secret. But it is one of the difficult sides of being an enchantress – having to tell people *no*.'

Snapdragon was now in a chatty mood. 'I could have cured the bird, but that all went wrong. My satchel was too full. I should never have tried to carry it up that tree, especially not with a bubble charm – they are so unreliable and precarious. But I was late. Trying to finish off too many spells. I was even carrying a thermos of tea and a couple of snacks wrapped in a white napkin. Those nice caramel biscuits Knox makes – you know the ones, Raven. And I was reading from the *Handy Guide to the Best Places and Times to Gather Plants of the Most Magical Variety*.'

She shook her head and Raven thought Grandma was now afflicted, like the rest of the family, with an inability to stick to the point. But she was hardly going to interrupt someone stuck inside a music box if they fancied a chat.

'Stupid. All my fault. Phials of almost-ready

magic, bits of magical plants, bits of non-magical stems and flowers, medical leaves and I think a family of woodlice, at least two black candles, the recently sloughed skin of a grass snake – I can't remember now what spell that was even for. And the tea.'

Snapdragon adjusted her position, bending her head low over her stretched-out legs, and carried on. 'Should have had a clear-out.'

'Grandma, Snapdragon, what do you mean?'

'I sailed higher than even cats can climb. I know that because there was one stretched out and I said hello as I passed. I was distracted thinking I must remember to tell the Maudlins. Their kittens kept escaping and you never knew where you'd find one next. I had settled into a nice steady bubble charm.'

Raven now kept very quiet. Snapdragon was piecing together her last moments. Was Raven finally going to solve the mystery of what had happened? Had she been attacked?

'It was the flowers I was after. I gather them and the roots every year. Valuable. The rarest of the rare. The pink variety of starlight moss. It grows from the topmost branches of some very ancient oak trees – the flowers hang, but only at the right time of year.'

'That's why it's called the hanging tree? Nothing to do with . . .'

'That's it exactly, my dear. I was just thinking how it would perfectly round off two little charms I was carrying. I was just finishing those spells, delighted knowing the bird would sing again. I was thinking how clever I had been getting that bubble charm to float me up high enough. And wondering if I'd have time for that tea and a cake before my class. You know what they say – pride comes before a fall. I completely flipped.'

'Someone upset you? Someone attacked you?'

'No, I flipped. I found myself quite upside down. I lost control of the bubble and was falling. Plunging out of the tallest tree in Beechy Wood. I had to act before I even had time to think.' She stifled a yawn.

Raven thought she heard footsteps and she dropped her voice to a whisper. 'What happened, Grandma?'

'Don't call me Grandma. Do you know, when I was very little, sometimes I just wanted to hide. Particularly from my older sister. She was better than me at everything.'

'Great-Aunt Agatha was better than you at magic?'

Raven was having difficulty even picturing stern and domineering Great-Aunt Agatha ever being a child.

'Especially magic.' Snapdragon gave the most enormous yawn. 'I perfected one spell when I was very young. I could make myself very, very small in an instant. But I never told her.' Snapdragon stretched and settled herself into her sleeping pose. 'Work hard and you can perfect any spell, Raven, remember that. If ever Agatha got cross, I'd annoy her by looking like I'd disappeared completely. I could do it in a flash and the music box was my favourite place to hide because it used to have a dancer in it, but that got broken off. I'm sure that was Agatha, although she never admitted it. I got so good at it, I could make myself vanish from anywhere and reappear in that music box. She never found me.'

'You sent yourself to this music box from the hanging tree?'

Snapdragon yawned in her sleeping pose. The black triangles began to twitch and close.

'I did dear. I was upside down, falling out of a tree and those charms spilling all over the place. Mixing magic is always a bad idea. It was a terrible disaster, but yes, I saved myself. I doubt even Agatha herself would have been able to do that.'

28. A Little Piece of Her Alive

Raven looked up to see a pair of green eyes staring right at her. She'd thought she'd heard a noise from the lane and had assumed it was probably one of the Twinhills kids heading home after Photography Club. But the cat had crept right up to her without her noticing, which was bad, but not as bad as when she turned and Morti was standing behind her as well. What had they seen?

'You were talking to someone in that music box? Is that magic?'

'Morti. I didn't—'

'It is, isn't it? I've scarcely ever seen magic being done. And your mum told us to come in the side gate, probably thought it safer than me coming through the house in case I stumbled on things I'm not supposed to see. And here you are in the garden, talking to a mini person.'

Morti crouched down next to her, looking at the intricate wooden box.

Raven hesitated for a moment, but felt she had abandoned Deny Everything a lifetime ago. 'I was talking to Snapdragon.'

'But she's . . . dead.' Morti's conker-coloured eyes grew round. 'Oh. Wow! Your grandma is a horcrux!'

Nightshade began a little wash.

'I have no idea how she managed to keep a little piece of herself alive in a music box, but I do know she wouldn't have murdered anyone to do it.'

'But, to be clear, she is dead?'

Nightshade paused as she reached for a hard-to-reach place on her back. 'Let's just say that magic is pretty complicated, and I suspect Raven doesn't actually know the answer.'

Morti looked at Raven, his eyes gleaming. 'Tell us in a minute what you were talking to her about, because you disappeared off and I didn't know if you knew – the Howling Hag's been up to her tricks again! Only went and smashed old Odorless's precious mug. Guess that means he's definitely not the Howling Hag. Unless it's a clever bluff to throw us off the scent.'

Raven wondered where to begin. 'But that wasn't the Howling Hag. It wasn't magic that moved that mug . . . it was Sam Carruthers.'

'Sam is the Howling Hag? You've gone and solved Operation Pickles without us?' Morti sounded more disappointed than impressed.

'What? No.'

Raven explained how she had bumped into Sam in Mr Odorless's office and brought them up to date with how Aaliyah had the incriminating stone and stolen money.

'Wow! So Aaliyah is the Howling Hag? Aaliyah is the terrifying witch who stuck a knife in Mr Pickles? Told you it'd be the least likely suspect!' Morti shook his head. 'But hang on . . . Sam and Aaliyah? They can't both be.' His face crumpled with the effort of working it out. 'Can they?'

'I asked Sam straight out if he was the Howling Hag. He wasn't giving much away, but he knows something. He said he it was his turn again and that he had to. He told me not to say anything and remember what happened to Mr Pickles. And he said *that's not how it works*. That's exactly what Aaliyah said to me.'

'Well, how does it work?' asked Morti. 'I mean, they can't all be magical.'

'Actually, I sort of think that might be how it's done,' said Raven, and told them what she'd talked to Snapdragon about, giving her theory of the Howling Hag's magical affinity being powerful mind control.

'OK, I think I've got it,' said Nightshade, giving up trying to clean a hard-to-reach place and leaping to her feet to sharpen her claws on the apple tree.

'What? A flea?' said Morti.

Nightshade gave him a slow, intense look with her green eyes. 'That would be a way to keep someone like Aaliyah from speaking out, wouldn't it – if she was made to steal the money and the stone? Told you at the beginning – secrets are power. Sometimes I reckon secrets are more powerful than magic.'

'Make it a secret everyone has to keep,' nodded Morti. 'That legend going about that the Howling Hag lures children into the woods to eat them and what happened to Mr Pickles, that would keep people in line. Sounds like all Miss Percy's class know a lot more about the Howling Hag than we do. We need to get one of them to talk. Hey! We could head to Board Games Club. It's on late. Doesn't start until after Photography Club. And all Miss Percy's class go. You might want to put your grandma somewhere safe first.' He nodded at the now silent music box.

Nightshade was shaking her head. 'Board Games Club hasn't run for weeks.'

'No, Morti's right. It's every week,' said Raven. 'Rookery goes. She'll be up there now. Mum gets cross because it goes on so late.'

'No,' said Nightshade. 'Believe me, I keep my whiskers to the ground. It's not been running for weeks. Makes me wonder where Rookery is right now?'

They all sat there in silence for a few moments, taking this in.

'Let's head up to the school, get a trace of them,' suggested Morti. 'Confront the class. Sounds like we might be heading to Operation Pickles Tertiary Phase.'

'Or,' said Nightshade, extending her claws, 'why don't I climb up the hanging tree and see what I can spot. Meet me there.' And she slipped away saying she'd be much faster on her own.

They began the long way around, down the path from the high street that eventually looped around the back of the school. They hadn't got far when they met Nightshade already coming back at a run. 'I think I've found them. She was already leading the way, loping ahead across the tangled, uneven ground, then turned to grumble at them. 'Do your paws actually have more than one speed? Just as well Morti's cleared this path, as you really need to get moving. Whiskers and white mice, you're going to want to see this. You need to be quick, but you also need to be really quiet.'

Morti and Raven followed as best they could, just about keeping sight of her black tail.

29. The Fire Ceremony

It was the sound that first told them something really odd was happening. The unmistakeable crackle of a large fire. Raven turned to Morti, but he had his finger on his lips reminding her they needed to be in stealth mode.

'How can a pair of young humans sound like a herd of elephants?' grumbled Nightshade. But it wasn't easy to be stealthy when walking through a dry, overgrown wood.

The sun was beginning to dip behind the trees

when they reached the clearing. In the gathering dusk, a group of small figures flitted in and out, collecting twigs and sticks and tossing them on eager flames. The Howling Hag's fire.

Their elongated shadows had great long fingers like claws, but the scariest thing was that they were all wearing masks. Masks identical to the one Raven had found hidden in her sister's room, with slits for eyes and dark hoods that covered their heads.

'What are they doing?' hissed Morti in a low voice. 'This is magic, right?'

Neither Raven nor Nightshade answered. They just watched from the shadows.

'Are all Miss Percy's class here?' asked Morti. 'Is Rookery here?'

Rookery was probably the tallest in the class, but in the twilight and with the figures flitting under the dappling shade of the trees and the red of the dying sun mixing with the glow of the fire, it was impossible to tell anyone apart.

Raven felt they were all thinking the same thing. One of them was the Howling Hag.

'What about the teachers?' said Nightshade.

'Mr Odorless is short enough,' answered Morti.

'Do you want me to try to get a little closer?' asked Nightshade.

Eventually, all the figures stopped bringing twigs to feed the blaze, and stood in a circle around it, the flames casting a distorting light. A new sound began. They started speaking, a low chanting, singing almost. Raven tried to make out exactly what they were saying. Was it a spell?

The figures linked hands and began to move slowly in a circle around the fire, the flickering flames dancing with them, and with the growing dusk and the sinking sun, the creepy shadows got even longer. It was like watching a dream. Except those masks made it a nightmare. They looked less than human. More like the ghosts of monsters.

The chanting was getting louder and Raven could make out words, sung to a familiar tune and repeated over and over.

'The Hag is out to get us, the Howling Hag's gonna eat us.

She will choose. Make it true.

Dance around the fire pit,

Someone's going to do it,

Do it, you. Or she'll eat us too.'

Then the chanting became less sing-song and grew louder and became the familiar chant: *'She's going to* trick *you. She's going to* get *you. She's going to* eat *you.'* Then abruptly the chanting stopped. And the dancing. But the fire flickered on. Then there was a screech and instead of dancing everyone was running in a circle around the flames, waving their arms above their heads and screaming. The flames were beginning to die and it was growing darker in the shadows of Beechy Wood.

Then they stopped so suddenly that Raven wondered if someone had given a secret instruction. She looked around. Was the Howling Hag here? She almost expected to see the arrival of a warty old woman in a pointy hat with a broomstick.

The flames were dulling to a red glow. There was a sudden silence, a moment of stillness. The glowing embers sent a spectral light over the whole clearing and on those masks. Everything was hushed.

'Are they waiting for something?' whispered Morti. All they could do was watch together, transfixed, lurking in the dark stillness of the surrounding beech trees waiting for what was going to happen next, hoping they wouldn't be spotted.

Raven thought one of the figures tossed something on to the embers, but it happened too quick to be sure. An enormous crack went up from the last remaining flames. Sparks flew in the direction of one of the masked figures and that figure hesitated, then darted forwards and pulled something from the very edge of the flames, drawing out a long, stout stick and holding it gingerly.

'I thought there was an epidemic of burnt fingers,' growled Nightshade. 'Now we know why.'

The figure was removing something from the stick. A slip of paper? Within seconds it was tossed back on the fire.

Then everyone melted into the shadows. The clearing was empty except for a lone figure who threw a bucket of water on to the remains of the fire, dousing the embers and sending up a grey cloud of smoke and ash.

All then it was just Raven, Morti and Nightshade left.

They stood in silence, finding it difficult to take in what they had just seen. Nightshade asked Raven if she still had the piece of paper she had snatched from the ash of the previous fire. Raven took it from her pocket and smoothed it so they could look at it again.

'I knew the burnt fingers were important,' said Morti. 'Didn't I say too many in Miss Percy's class had burnt fingers? What were they picking out of the fire?'

'I guess this is how it works,' said Nightshade. 'One of them, every week picks the curse out of the fire. It's a key part of why no one could tell how the curses were being done. It's a different person each time. They have to do their curse without anyone spotting. No suspicion falls on one person, but everyone is involved. Everyone is implicated if they speak out. Very clever. It's quite brilliant, actually.'

'Worthy of one of your worst cases of sinister sorcerers gone bad?' asked Morti. He prodded a dirty finger at the singed scrap of paper they hadn't been able to make sense of before. 'So is this one of the curses?'

> orld's Best Headte
> ash i
> mber Mr Pi

'We didn't think it was a spell,' explained Nightshade. 'We were right! It's an instruction.'

'I get it! This one must have said something like: *Pinch Mr Odorless's World's Best Head Teacher mug and smash it*. I reckon that last line is a warning if you don't do it right. *Remember Mr Pickles*.' Morti's eyes were shining. 'Well, this is a whole lot more interesting than Board Games Club.'

30. The Secret Shelf

All the next day at school Raven had looked for
signs of what was to come next from the Howling Hag. But the whole day went calmly. Raven
was told off twice by Miss Sunny for not paying
attention. But how could you focus on multiplication
when you knew for sure that someone at school was
a witch?

Or were they?

Raven's thoughts had stayed on the clearing in the
wood, seeing those masked figures dancing. She,

Morti and Nightshade had followed the evidence. They knew a lot. Raven could imagine how the Howling Hag's hold might have started – people being invited to join in with something that sounded fun, a little daring, like a secret club; identities kept under wraps. A couple of small tricks to begin with. But did it really matter how things had started? What mattered was that once people were involved . . . hadn't Nightshade said that secrets could be more powerful than magic?

Raven could see that was true. Because even now it felt like Operation Pickles was back to Alpha Phase, because there was still no answer to the big question: how were they going to break the curse on the school and stop the Howling Hag if they could simply not work out who he or she was?

She was just looking at, but not reading, *The Unfortunate History of the Most Unlucky Magical Folk and Occurrences*. It was a small book with a long title, which was in tiny type to fit on the front cover. It was known to the Charmings simply as *The Unlucky*. The pages were delicate and soft with use. Like all of the Charmings' magical books, it had been touched by the thumbs of magical Charmings going back hundreds of years.

Raven's first thought had been to quiz her sister.

But she remembered what Sam had said when she'd asked him about the Howling Hag's identity. *Wouldn't we all like to know that!* Did any of Miss Percy's class actually know who was giving the secret instructions?

'Did I ever tell you how I discovered my affinity for magic?' asked Mum, interrupting Raven's thoughts. She must have guessed that Raven wasn't actually reading. She removed her glasses and chewed one of the ends, then disappeared into the kitchen without waiting for an answer.

Snapdragon had told Raven someone was making the Howling Hag up. But someone had to invent the curses and write those instructions and leave them in a hollow log on the edge of the fire. Someone had sent a clear message to anyone not following the Howling Hag's instructions with a pair of scissors right in the middle of Mr Pickles' belly.

It was all so very clever. And it didn't even need to involve magic.

Nightshade had talked more than once about the power of secrets. And Raven had realized the power of rumours in getting people to believe things that weren't true.

Raven was still going over everything when her mum returned and placed, quite amazingly, a plate of cookies and a glass of milk on her desk, an invitation for Raven to sit. Rookery had made the cookies as a welcome-home gift for Dad, but he was still stuck at the conference.

'I bet you assumed I always knew I was going to be magical,' said Mum.

Raven nodded and slipped a cookie from the plate.

'I don't think I've ever told you how I found my affinity.'

Raven knew for sure that Mum had not told her this. Raven suspected this was because Mum thought the news would just make Raven sad.

Because everything she tried to do, despite all her hours spent with her books and all the patient teaching, never made her feel any magic. The books would all be passed down to Rookery and then to the magical family she might have one day.

'I found out because of my mother, your grandmother.'

'Snapdragon worked out what your magic was?' Raven wished someone could simply tell her. Just knowing would be enough. She could wait for it. If only someone would spot it for what it was. But she was so close to resigning herself to it never happening.

'Snapdragon could be a little . . . slapdash.'

'I thought you said you couldn't be slapdash with magic.' Raven had begun to nibble the cookie, but now took a big bite. 'Is slapdash why Snapdragon had her accident?'

'We were talking about my magic,' said Finch hurriedly, avoiding as usual any discussion of Snapdragon's accident. 'The reason I knew what my magic was going to be was because I lived in a house full of experimental charms, half-completed spells, or spells that had misfired and Snapdragon was meaning to fix. Or objects where magic had fallen on the wrong things. It was like living in a mixed-up, crazy, illogical, multicoloured, confusing place. I suffered a lot from headaches.'

Mum went on. 'I tried to sort them out, make sense of things, restore order. And I had a knack for working out what she'd meant to do . . . where she'd gone wrong and how it might be fixed. And sometimes we'd work together and straighten it out. It made Dandelion Cottage a much more soothing place to live.'

'And that's how you became a curse breaker?'

'Eventually. Once the Elysee heard of my talent, I was taken on as an apprentice.'

Snapdragon was a brilliant if slightly accident-prone witch. Mum, like Rookery, found her magic so effortless she'd never had to think about it at all. Raven would not have felt so full of failure if she hadn't been born into quite such an extraordinarily skilled magical family. And she kept reading about the many magical people who were, frankly, terrible at magic, and caused far more problems than they ever solved.

'I didn't know until recently that Great-Aunt Agatha was even more skilled at magic than Snapdragon when they were children. Snapdragon told me she loved to do one piece of magic that confused her sister. It turned out to be very useful, didn't it, because she could do it even when faced with real danger. I guess I just have to get used to the fact it's me who's the odd one out.'

Mum tipped her head to one side. 'I don't think I know that story. But you were always so close to your grandma.'

Raven drank her milk and absent-mindedly took another cookie, realizing she'd almost given away the fact she'd been disturbing Snapdragon in her sleep. She didn't want to be in trouble for that on top of everything else.

Mum had brought her these biscuits that were actually meant for Dad. Was that because Mum was about to finally say what no one ever said out loud? Was she using them to soften the blow of telling Raven she'd never be magic?

'How old were you when you actually knew you were going to be a brilliant sorcerer?' Raven had tried to keep her voice steady and hated the way it came out so choked and trembly. But she'd had a tough few days and the last thing she needed right now was to be made to face up to her lack of magic. 'You were younger than me when you started to fix all of Snapdragon's broken magic, weren't you? You must have been. Because you started working as an apprentice when you were sixteen.'

'Well, yes, but I—'

'So you must have known long before. It's OK. I know what's coming,' she sighed. *Being magical isn't everything. Dad's not magical, I . . .*'

Mum looked uncomfortable and Raven could tell that whatever she'd planned to say when she'd brought in the milk and cookies, it wasn't coming out right.

'You don't believe I've got magic, do you?' Raven sighed, in a quivery voice, biting her lip to stop the tears coming. 'There. I have finally said it. I wish you would just say it. Then we could all move on and I could stop reading these ridiculous ancient books and living in a dream where I just spend my life waiting and hope my magic is going to come.'

'I wasn't . . . I'm saying it's hard for anyone involved in the magical world. It's hard for Rookery to control her magic,' Mum said. 'And for me to know she has a dangerous life ahead of her, especially after what happened to—'

'I know how hard it is for Rookery.' Raven could not stop herself snapping. 'At least she's useful. Bringing kites down from trees, letting the weakest girls score winning goals and tripping up the bullies. Those difficulties are better than not having any magic at all.'

The second the words were out, Raven regretted snitching on her sister. After all, her sister was hardly the only one who was failing at the Golden Rule of keeping magic a secret.

'Rookery's doing magic at school?' Mum's voice was anxious.

It was already too late, but Raven tried walking away. Mum laid a hand on her shoulder. Raven shrugged it off.

'I believe you and Rookery will always make good decisions in life. That's the main thing I will always try to teach you. Life is really not all about magic.'

'Well, cheers for the pep talk,' Raven snapped.

'Because, basically, that is the same as saying you don't believe I have magic. Honestly, you try to keep so much from us. Why don't you just come out and say I don't have magic? Why don't you talk to us properly and tell us the truth, like exactly what happened to Snapdragon?'

Mum let out a very long sigh. 'It's not because I don't want to. There is plenty I don't know. I wish I did have all the answers. We will never know what happened to Snapdragon and that is tough. We could never find a single trace of her. I wish we did have some idea of what went wrong with someone as powerful as Snapdragon. I can't stop imagining it was something terrible.'

'Well, not quite no trace.'

Mum suddenly went very, very still.

'Raven. What you said . . . a moment ago you said something you only just found out . . . do you mean . . .' Her voice was very low. 'Raven. Have you spoken to Snapdragon since she died?'

31. DEVIOUS AND MANIPULATIVE

'I'm sorry!' Raven said quickly. 'I knew I probably shouldn't wake her. Snapdragon is so tired, but last time she seemed keen to chat, I ...'

But she could not even think of an excuse. She just went to fetch the music box.

She'd known she'd get into trouble for this, but why did it have to be so soon? Snapdragon was so helpful, the only one who ever gave straight answers.

She went to the bottom of her wardrobe and shifted aside a pile of clothes she was supposed to

have put properly into drawers and on to hangers.

The music box wasn't there.

She frantically shifted the clothes, her heart seeming to slow and her whole body turning cold. It had to be here. She went through everything again until she became aware of Rookery standing in the doorway, watching with a stillness and a silence and with her almost-yellow eyes.

And, on the hand gripping the doorframe, were two plasters.

'The Howling Hag made me do it,' she whispered.

'You've given her the music box? Where is it? What have you done?' demanded Raven, trying to keep her voice under control when it wanted to spill out in rage and in fear. Because this could not be happening. Rookery could not have been the one to pull an instruction out of the fire – to steal the music box. 'How did the Howling Hag even know about the music box?' she asked, her voice steely.

But even as Rookery answered with a shake of her head, Raven thought she might have the answer. She cursed herself for opening the beautiful old box in the garden, so close to the busy footpath. Why hadn't she simply left Snapdragon where she had been, perfectly safe and undisturbed up at Knox's?

Rookery looked not just upset, but guilty and

terrified. 'You have to do what the Howling Hag says. She threatens to lure the kids into the woods. Look what happened to Mr Pickles. Who knows what she might do next.'

Raven's mouth was dry, but she was thinking quickly. She had to remind herself her sister had no idea of the secret contained in the music box.

'Have you any idea who he or she really is? Has anyone? How do we get the music box back? When did you hand it over?'

Then Mum was suddenly standing behind Rookery, and all Raven's guilt flooded in again.

'Are you looking for Snapdragon's old musical box?' asked Mum. 'Because I'm sure Knox has that. Why do you want it?'

Raven swallowed hard, her heart thudding in her chest. Because even in all her confusion, she was able to see things weren't quite right. Mum asking why she wanted the music box could only mean that Mum didn't know what was inside . . .

There was no way Raven could break the news and in the same breath tell her the box was lost. Not just lost, but now in the hands of someone very devious and manipulative. Snapdragon was inside that box and had now been kidnapped. It was too awful.

'We can't tackle the Howling Hag,' whispered Rookery.

'Of course we can get that music box back,' Raven reassured her sister who was chewing her lip anxiously. 'We just have to be smarter than the Howling Hag.'

She had one slim chance to cover up this whole nightmarish mistake and to put things right. She needed Nightshade and Morti.

'You know you just said you'd trust me to make the right decisions?' she said to Mum, grabbing Rookery as she edged past. 'Well, I need you to trust me now. We'll explain everything later. Rookery and I have something we have to sort out.'

32. Sneaking About and Listening

They left Sundial Cottage together at a run.

'My instructions were to leave it in the dragon tree,' said Rookery. 'Let's hope we're not too late.'

Raven's heart leapt with hope at the thought that there might still be time.

She hoped the Howling Hag simply wanted the box as it was pretty, old and valuable . . . but what Raven really dreaded was that whoever might have been watching her in the garden might have worked out its magical secret. Did the Howling Hag plan to

get hold of Snapdragon for her magic?

Because there was one thing Raven was beginning to suspect – the Howling Hag didn't have any magic of her own. They had to get that music box back before the Hag found out she had a miniature witch at her mercy and tried to use Snapdragon's magic.

They still had a chance.

There was too much to explain as they ran along the high street, sprinted past the school and turned at the fingerpost sign to head into Beechy Wood.

There was only one thing Rookery needed to know right now – that it was imperative they get back the music box, because Snapdragon was now really small and inside it. Raven explained that Snapdragon didn't die. She'd just got really clobbered by a load of spells and put herself under some sort of enchantment to escape, but now seemed to be trapped under it, and that Raven had only just worked out that Mum never knew.

'We need to get the music box back off the Howling Hag.'

She almost tripped over Nightshade prowling on the edge of the wood, whiskers twitching at a passing bird as if she had nothing more important in mind than seeking something fluttery and feathery to have fun with.

Yet she did seem to possess a knack of appearing when Raven needed her help. Raven quickly updated her with the terrible developments and watched as Nightshade scampered straight off to fetch Morti.

Raven looked at her sister and told her that, yes, there was a lot more she needed to catch up on.

Rookery did little other than raise her eyebrows. 'I can see that, but tell me later, let's keep our breath for beating the Howling Hag to the dragon tree.'

The straggling grass and snatching brambles hardly slowed Rookery, who raced ahead along the overgrown path. It was all Raven could do to keep up as her taller sister ploughed on ahead, tearing through tall nettles, not letting anything slow her frantic pace as she made for the small secret hollow in their favourite tree, their hidey-hole of childhood.

Would the music box still be safely there, or had the Howling Hag got to it first? Raven hoped they were in time.

And she kept reminding herself that the Howling Hag was not a real witch. It was an illusion conjured up from carefully spread rumours, tricks to convince people there was a witch moving things about at will without anyone ever being able to explain it. Smoke and mirrors stirring up a lot of spooked-up fear.

There wasn't really a powerful sorcerer behind all of this.

She hoped.

Yet the Howling Hag *was* real enough, even if she wasn't an ancient witch come back to life. She'd used that fire ceremony to get control, made the kids believe it was some sort of spell, something they could not escape without retribution. Now the whole school whispered her name in fear.

So who was she?

Rookery reached the dragon tree first, but Raven was in time to watch her plunge her hand into a dark space in the tree trunk and grope around.

Raven waited, her fists clenched, breathing hard from the run and from the tension. Every single moment the Howling Hag was always a step ahead of them. But hopefully this time they had got there first. Any second now and Rookery would turn around with the music box safe in her hands. Raven hopped from one leg to the other.

Her sister's look told the story as she turned.

'It's gone.' A look of distress crossed Rookery's face and she bit her lip hard. 'The Howling Hag must have fetched it already. She's got Snapdragon.'

'There's no such person as the Howling Hag,' Raven answered stoutly. 'It's someone pretending, getting people at school to do stuff. Silly to begin with, but all designed to make it look like witchcraft. But it's more than fun and games now. She's growing powerful – people do everything she asks. Now she's got Snapdragon.'

'If it's someone just trying to scare people, perhaps she'll just bring it back,' suggested Rookery. 'When she realizes she's got something magical.'

Rookery was far more hopeful than Raven.

Those who believed in magic could be jealous of the abilities and the power it gave some people. The Howling Hag's games had given her a little taste of that power, and now she had the chance to seize more.

If Raven had read the Howling Hag right, there was no chance at all she would meekly hand Snapdragon back. The Howling Hag might force their grandma to do magic, magic that might make Snapdragon weaker, might even kill her. 'Snapdragon is very weak and just opening that box seemed to make her even more tired. She's in real trouble. We need to think, Rookery,' Raven said desperately. 'Who is it?'

Rookery's eyes were wide and she was shaking. 'I don't know any more than anyone else about who the Howling Hag really is. We've lost, Raven.'

'Hey!' The cry made them both turn to see Morti scrabbling along the lane holding a short lead, roped into taking Titus for a walk again. 'Nightshade told me. Kidnapping your grandma! She's gone too far this time. We have to get your grandma back. Meeting at HQ now.'

Raven looked at her sister. 'Will you help us?'

Rookery nodded without even hesitating. 'Of course. I'll go and get Bianca too. We need all the help we can get and she's full of great ideas.'

Raven wasn't sure letting everyone in on the secret was such a brilliant plan, but frankly, Rookery was right, they needed all the help they could get. Rookery didn't wait a second but started sprinting back along the path.

Raven and Morti headed for the den. It was difficult to think straight, yet it had never been more important. Raven felt her spirits wilt. Rookery was right; the Howling Hag had won.

As Titus got nearer with his menacing slobber, there was a noise above them. Raven saw Nightshade shooting up into the branches high above. Titus jerked the lead right out of Morti's hand trying to go after her, but she disappeared into the thick foliage. Morti grabbed the end of the lead and tied it to a low branch, tossing Titus a big stick to chew on. Titus threw himself on to the ground and started attacking it.

'Where's Carsen?' asked Raven.

'Dunno. Looking for Titus, I expect. Just found him in the wood. But I came to find you. You think the Hag knows your grandma is in that box?' Morti asked, as Nightshade dared slink a little lower.

Raven told them the conclusion she'd reached. 'I'm sure the Howling Hag has no magic. She's done all this so it looks as if she can do magic. And now,' she finished glumly, 'if we don't find her and get that music box back, she *will* have magic. We have to stop her. But only if we can work out who it is,' said Raven desperately, looking at her friends.

'You gotta say the Howling Hag is clever,' nodded Morti. 'So come on, let's go over the suspects again. You caught Sam right in the act of pinching that mug. I can imagine him being the one to organize big scary fire ceremonies with everyone learning terrifying chants and wearing awful masks so no one sees who gets the next curse to carry out. Easier than believing it's Aaliyah.'

And then a voice rang out. 'Oh, so this is where you hang out. Finally! We've caught you.' It was Sam.

33. Secret Headquarters

In fact, it wasn't only Sam. Raven could not quite believe the number of faces that ducked under the low branches that concealed the den from prying eyes.

Sam was followed by Henry, Carsen, Ella and even Aaliyah, all wide-eyed as they slipped into the den.

Ella immediately began commenting on everything, from the big slab of table to the tree trunks arranged around it. 'It's not a secret den – it's a whole secret house!' she squeaked.

Sam headed for the xylophone and began to bash out a few notes. 'Your secret headquarters weren't secret enough for us,' he grinned. 'You weren't that difficult to follow. You and Morti have been spying on all of us, haven't you? It's about time you told us what you're up to.'

'We guess it's about the Howling Hag,' said Henry, taking a tree-trunk seat next to Raven. He was wearing shorts, and Raven couldn't resist inspecting his prize-winning knobbly knees.

'You've worked out what's been going on, haven't you? We all just went along with it – the fire ceremony and doing sneaky things to make it look like curses. But you're trying to stop it,' said Carsen. He had brought a tennis ball and started to toss it from hand to hand, ignoring the fact that Titus's ears began to twitch as his eyes followed the ball longingly.

'It was fun for a bit,' agreed Sam. 'We kind of liked doing dares, seeing what you can get away with, seeing if we could make everyone think it was magic and there was a witch cursing the school.'

'But she freaked us all out with what happened to Mr Pickles,' said Ella.

'And the little kids are getting terrified now,' said Sam. 'They believe the school has really been cursed by an evil witch who is lurking in the woods and threatening to eat them. Plus the Howling Hag just takes the credit for everything, but it's us taking the risks!'

'Every time some tiny thing happens everyone says it's the Howling Hag,' said Ella. 'She's getting way too powerful. Even for a witch.'

'We think it's time we stopped,' said Carsen.

'We're fed up with it,' said Sam.

'And we think you've got a plan,' finished Henry.

'Is that what you're up to?' asked Aaliyah.

'Of course we've got a plan,' Morti said, then stopped, overwhelmed by the number of people looking at him. Raven could tell he was wishing they knew more than they actually did. 'Would anyone like crisps?' he offered. From behind a pile of logs he produced a stash.

Raven chewed her lip. Unfortunately, pretty much all their main suspects were now here, in their secret headquarters, and their cover was completely blown. Perhaps they really weren't good at this at all. Which was a terrible shame, as everyone had come to them for help. But surely together they could finally stop the Howling Hag? If everyone stood up to her, she would lose her power over them. Raven had to believe they could win.

More faces appeared under the low-hanging

branches. Rookery was here with Bianca, who had brought two whole tins of posh biscuits. There was a quick shuffle as everyone moved on from Morti's crushed crisps.

Sam munched his way through two biscuits while giving a flourish of notes on the xylophone. 'We're all in. What do we do?'

'Well, she's clever,' said Morti. 'And she's been careful and people really are scared. But we don't believe she's an actual witch.' He winked at Raven. 'Whose curse was killing Mr Pickles?'

No one spoke up.

'I reckoned that one was the Howling Hag herself,' said Sam. 'Or *him*self, I guess? But we need to work out who it is before we can do anything.'

'But we can stop her or him telling us we have to play these cruel tricks on each other, can't we?' said Ella. 'You're sure she's not a real witch? You're sure she's not going to trick the little children into the woods?'

'That's just a story,' reassured Morti kindly. 'And of course we can stop her.'

'But how?' asked Bianca. 'If you don't know who it is?'

'Well,' said Morti, looking about him, 'we do have a main suspect, we just can't pin anything on him. We think it might be Mr Odorless.'

'Mr Odorless!' Even strutting Sam looked stricken. 'We didn't know it was going to mean catching Mr Odorless.'

A collective gasp went around, reminding Raven of when Nightshade had first delivered the news that she and Morti were going to have to investigate their head.

Morti explained how they thought he might have got so desperate to beat Fivetors at something, he'd go to almost any lengths. 'Trouble is, all detectives follow the evidence and so far, we've got nothing on him.'

Aaliyah put her head on one side. 'So how do we get evidence?'

'What evidence are we looking for?' asked Carsen, still playing with the tennis ball, and Titus's eyes still watching it intently.

'We know the latest curse,' said Raven in a small voice. 'It was to steal something,' she said quietly. 'Whoever the Howling Hag is, they have something very precious that belongs to me.'

'Sorry to hear that,' said Henry.

It felt pretty strange to suddenly have all their suspects now flip to the other side and be part of Operation Pickles, yet it felt like the right move. Particularly having Rookery involved. Her sister was doing what she usually did, staying silent and almost motionless, slightly away from everyone else, almost invisible in the shadowy branches at the very darkest part of the den. But Raven didn't need Rookery to speak. She knew exactly how she would feel if they didn't get back that music box. And that meant only one thing.

'We need to get into Mr Odorless's house and search it,' said Raven, quietly but insistently. Her suggestion was met with silence.

If Mr Odorless had that music box, all they needed to do was find it. They could rescue Snapdragon and it would give them the proof they needed to stop him. They could not afford to fail.

'Well, I guess if you're going to search his house,' began Carsen brightly, 'I'd go now. He's out, and –' he pointed at Titus – 'we've got the hell hound.'

Raven's mouth went dry. *Do it right now?*

The thought filled her with a quiet terror. She reckoned she was about to do something far worse than any of the curses the Howling Hag had set anyone. Yet she was surprised to discover that she was already on her feet. She had to stop Neg and close that black hole of fear inside of her before it even opened, because it would stop her legs carrying her towards the one chance to save her grandmother.

34. Lifting The Curse

Raven had completely forgotten Nightshade was there – she had been so still up in the branches above the den. But the moment she headed back along the path to the high street and a job that needed to be done, there was her familiar black shadow, slinking in behind.

'Nightshade! Nice to have company on a dangerous mission.'

'Yes, well I haven't done one today, I need the practice.'

'Who would want a life to be all salmon and snoozing?'

With Nightshade alongside her, Raven walked almost confidently and they were soon, too soon, only a few steps away from Tidy House.

The trick was not to let her imagination get ahead of her, not to picture herself being caught inside Mr Odorless's house. He'd be tending to his sunflowers ahead of the judging of the tallest sunflower competition on Sunday. He wouldn't be long. But she could do this, break in, find her music box, save Snapdragon and stop Mr Odorless spooking the school.

Nightshade was twitching her tail. 'If you were a cat, you could climb up to that small first-floor window that's open. Want me to do it?'

'Thanks, Nightshade, but I need to do this myself.'

Raven opened the well-oiled gate and shut it smoothly behind her before making her way along the bleached path, between the waxy flowers planted in regimental rows and round to the back of the house.

'Well, you seem to have conquered most of your fears, Raven Charming. I thought it might be mostly fear holding you back. Losing Snapdragon in a magical accident must have been terrible. But this is brave, Raven.'

'Thanks, but I don't need a reminder at exactly this moment.'

'You're never going to fit through that window.'

'No need. Carsen gave me this.' She opened her hand to reveal an iron key and unlocked the back door quietly before stepping inside. Nightshade padded softly in behind her as she turned and locked it again. They were in the kitchen, where, unsurprisingly, not even an upturned mug sat on the polished draining board.

The logical step would be to search the kitchen first. Be quick and organized, before she even had chance to think about what she was doing. Yet, she found herself wandering, a small flare of worry already burning inside her as she saw why Nightshade had been so confident Mr Odorless wasn't hiding evidence of a secretive magical life. There was nothing here – no magical artefacts, no spell book or half-tried charm, not so much as a stray beginner's scroll. Maybe she should have trusted the cat to have done a thorough job. Maybe she needn't have come at all. Maybe she could just leave. But no. She thought of everyone waiting with Morti back at the den. They wanted the Howling Hag stopped and it had to be Mr Odorless, but they needed proof. They needed that music box.

Raven trod carefully across the thick, pea-green carpet of the living room and headed up the stairs, Nightshade padding softly behind her. Nightshade said everyone had secrets. What was Mr Odorless's?

She prodded open a door upstairs. Spare bedroom. Empty, as if no one ever came to stay.

Bathroom next. Nightshade followed close, her big green eyes gleaming up at Raven. Single neatly folded towel. Single toothbrush. The house felt as if it was closing in on her and she had to fight an urge to run back outside.

This house seemed to be giving her a glimpse of her own future. Was this how she might live if she found her magic? Too afraid to invite anyone to stay because of having too many secrets to keep? Was that what having magic did for you – made you lonely?

But this home wasn't in the least like the friendly bustle of Sundial or Dandelion Cottage. They were houses lived in by sorcerers. Maybe there were many choices you might make that led to what your house looked like, or even how many friends wanted to come and visit. The Maudlins, for instance, liked white walls and things you daren't touch, even though Bianca loved inviting people to her parties.

'You're sensing something, aren't you?' said Nightshade, rubbing around her legs.

Raven nodded, thinking how tough it must be that people would never know the part Nightshade had played, teaching them how to be good detectives, giving them the courage to do things like . . . break into her head's house.

'You've been brilliant, Nightshade,' she said. 'It's unfair that no one will know.'

'Ah well, as Morti would say, Operation Pickles is reaching a critical phase and what's important is that the Howling Hag does not win.'

Nightshade had searched this house already and Raven really did trust the cat not to have missed anything. Somehow the house seemed to be telling her that the music box was not here. She had failed. Again. She should just go.

It almost felt as if the house was talking to her, whispering that she wasn't going to find the crucial evidence and rescue Snapdragon, because she wasn't the magical one. She was the one that wasn't good enough.

She had one more door to push open. This led to a bedroom that looked out over the garden, towards the school and on towards Beechy Wood. It contained a single bed with a white cover, a slim wooden wardrobe and a chest of drawers that doubled as a bedside table, on which sat a spare pair of glasses. She tried to concentrate on slowing her thundering heart. Blood was rushing in her ears as she had a familiar bolt of fear at the thought of taking the next step – especially as the next step would mean setting foot in Mr Odorless's bedroom. She hovered in the doorway. She wasn't good enough. She would always be second best.

'Call this searching?' Nightshade's voice interrupted her thoughts. 'Thought I did a better job with my paws and lack of opposable thumbs.'

Nightshade was right. Raven had to remind herself of why she was here. She should open that wardrobe door, poke about under the bed. And then it wasn't even fear that was stopping her. She realized she strongly wanted to close her eyes and listen. *Listen?* No, she meant *think*.

Instead of rummaging through everything before her time ran out, she simply stood there and thought about the first time she had found the music box. In the midst of her grief not long after Snapdragon's unfortunate accident, Raven had found herself wandering up the twisting stairs of Dandelion Cottage. She had peeped inside the box; Snapdragon had not even woken.

Every moment she stood here, every step further into this house, seemed to take her closer to knowing

Mr Odorless. The feeling was partly at the back of her throat, like a tingling, but mostly deep inside of her, where she needed to push aside that horrible dark hollow that lived there.

'What is it, Raven? It's something, I can tell.' Nightshade was looking up at her and blinking with her big wise eyes. Her voice was strange, as if Raven's ears were muffled.

She had found Snapdragon by listening, sort of. She listened now, recalling how when she'd opened the box, she'd had a feeling, sort of sad, confused, but mostly just very, very tired, which must be pretty much exactly as Snapdragon felt, turned into a miniature version of herself and trapped inside a box.

She closed her eyes and she remembered how Nightshade had said everyone had a secret. Mr Odorless desperately wanted Twinhills to win at something, because Fivetors was best at everything. That wasn't a secret, everyone knew that. But there was something more.

She started to feel something, partly in her fingers, but strangely, it wasn't her own feelings she was reaching for. This was deeper, and sadder. Nightshade was pawing at her leg. She shut the door to Mr Odorless's bedroom.

She felt dizzy, she gripped the banister, overwhelmed with those uncomfortable feelings of wanting to be the best at something. She wanted to push those feelings away, but even more, she wanted to understand.

It wasn't the feeling of not being good enough, but of not being *worthy*. That was the word that came to her from the voice. *Voice?* Yes, it was as if a voice was whispering all around her.

Raven made it to the bottom of the stairs and to the sitting room, sweating now, and almost sank into a big green armchair. *No, Raven.* She had to force her knees not to collapse, because Mr Odorless would be back soon.

She felt eyes staring at her and turned in startled alarm. It was only Nightshade. The cat said something, a word she didn't understand. It sounded like *scryer*. But she focused on the word *secret* as she gripped the back of a single chair tucked under a small table where someone might eat alone, every day. She felt more than just second best, in the air that now felt thick and heavy, and burnt the back of her throat, she could detect a yearning. The feelings were getting too loud.

Nightshade placed a paw gently on her leg and that touch helped. Raven felt the voices quieten, made her remember why she was breaking into her terrifying head teacher's house. Reminded her that she had to hurry.

She let her gaze wander for anywhere a secret could be hidden, the music box carefully placed, even a room where magic was clandestinely practised. A thick carpet covered the whole floor. No trapdoor. And Snapdragon wasn't here. She knew it. Because she could not hear her.

There was no evidence here. They'd got it wrong and that meant she was no nearer to recovering her grandma from the Howling Hag's clutches.

She turned to say something to Nightshade and the cat was no longer there. Gone. Abandoned, Raven's thoughts sank inwards. But there was a secret here. She felt it.

Raven went to the polished dresser and opened a drawer.

And she discovered Mr Odorless's secret in just the same second as a sound made her turn. Mr Odorless was standing right there in the room, his fists clenched and his strange, flat face turning slowly purple.

35. Consequences

I hadn't liked to leave her.

My job had been lookout cat. And I'd messed up.

I've seen someone go into a trance before. Magical people don't always know how to control their powers – or extra senses, whatever you want to call them – and unfortunately, going into Mr Odorless's house like that, all senses firing, she'd been pretty overcrowded by feelings. I could see what she was doing even if she didn't know it herself.

Raven could read the sort of traces people leave on treasured objects that they've held over and over.

At least I'd spotted she'd lost all track of time and we were going to need some help.

My plan was a swift exit through the open upstairs window. A lot higher than ideal. I teetered before I jumped, knowing I was going to have to make a near-impossible landing even for my nimble paws – a minimum of two paws on top of that narrow wall far below. Any less than two and I'd end up in a tangled and undignified heap at the bottom of the wall. And, just to be clear, don't believe any of that nonsense about cats having nine lives. We have exactly the same lives as anybody else. Which isn't the handiest thing to find yourself thinking about as you leap from a tiny high window.

Even that thing about cats always landing on their feet is a bit of a struggle to live up to. But there wasn't too much unseemly scrambling, and I'd done it in the nick of time – Mr Odorless was bustling up the high street on his short little legs.

I ran as fast as I could, wanting to get help and quickly return to Tidy House. Maybe I could get that anger directed at me and give Raven a chance to escape. After all, we have all the evidence we needed that Mr Odorless was definitely a dog person. I knew just the kind of help I needed ...

As soon as I could I was slipping in the front door again, just as Mr Odorless was realizing his house was not as empty as he was expecting.

'Raven Charming.'

The words came out low and menacing instead of his usual bellow, although his fists were clenched as if he was itching to hit something. 'Why is your family always at the heart of any trouble? What are you doing in my house?'

Poor Raven was completely frozen. Mr Odorless's face was turning more and more purple, a vein pulsing on his forehead.

I assessed my strategy. Which would be more effective? Rubbing around the legs and soft big eyes? Or a full-on menacing claw to the bottom of the leg? That one is a pretty much a dead cert to stop anyone in their tracks.

Or ... I looked for a precariously placed vase or anything valuable I might break to distract him, because Raven was not moving. Or speaking.

To be honest, there isn't very much you can say when you're caught breaking into your head teacher's house to try to prove they are a thief and a witch.

I advanced, making the decision to throw myself on him in full ninja mode. But then it occurred to me that if the assault failed, it was pretty sure to put him in an even uglier mood. So, at the very last second, I went for the rub around the leg option.

One thing I will say for this last-ditch switch of tactics: it certainly stopped old Mr Odorless in his tracks. We locked eyes just as the familiar sound of the slathering beast reached my ears. I never thought I would be relieved to hear the approach of the hell hound. But attached to the other end of the straining leash was Morti Scratch, wheezing as heavily as Titus. And right on cue.

I hadn't had to dash far along the high street to find him. He'd already noticed Raven was taking longer than she ought and was on his way to help. Now the leg-rubbing technique truly paid off. Titus lunged at me and the hound's lead tangled perfectly around Mr Odorless's legs. Luckily Morti let go of the other end just as the head staggered and went crashing to the floor. I sidestepped Titus and dashed outside to the top of my favourite wall, where I waited at a safe distance from the slathering jaws, my tail not even dangling.

The mangy brute's barking frenzy was obscuring what was being said, but I got the gist. It went from a lot of shouting at Raven to a lot of barking from Titus and a whole load of implausible excuses from Morti.

'Oh Raven! Thanks for coming back for Titus's ball, but you wouldn't have found it, because guess what?' He produced a tooth-marked rubber ball from his pocket. 'Wasted journey. Shall I just give Titus back to you, sir, or—'

'What is this girl doing in my house?' said Mr Odorless. It's difficult to maintain your level of anger when your dog is outdoing you. Odorless gave Titus the evil eye and then did all our ears a favour by tossing the small white rug into the kitchen and shutting the door.

'And where is Carsen? What are you doing with my dog, Scratch?'

'Just helping out. Carsen was running and twisted his ankle. He's in total agony. So we thought we'd do him and you a favour and walk Titus, only I know he likes his ball and—'

'You abandoned Carsen in agony and came back here to retrieve a ball?'

'Er – well, he got better.' Morti shifted through the gears impeccably. 'But, you are right. Wasn't nice of us to abandon him like that. We should go.' He grabbed Raven and tossed the ball to Mr Odorless.

'Luckily you're back now, aren't you sir?' He yanked Raven out of the back door and slammed it shut after them. He wiped his brow, where a sheen of nervous sweat glistened.

'That was a close one,' he said, then looked at Raven. 'I sure hope you've got the goods on Mr Odorless, because everyone is waiting.'

36. WHO IS THE HOWLING HAG?

Mr Odorless was not the Howling Hag.

Raven did not have the music box and I trusted her to have found it if it had been there. Even my paws felt sluggish at the thought that we were walking back to a waiting bunch of expectant wannabe detectives with the news that the big conclusion was wrong. What were we going to tell them?

I'd hoped by now we would be getting close to answers.

I'd told Morti the way to investigate a magical crime was the same as any crime. But I'd forgotten that lesson myself. As we walked I realized we'd allowed ourselves to get completely sidetracked by thinking we were looking for someone out for revenge. Someone magical. But when you stripped away all the stories, all the fakery, what were you left with? What did anyone stand to gain from spooking up Twinhills? Was there a pattern? A motive, that was what we were missing. That was what I had forgotten and this was what I considered as I padded along the hot pavement. Morti, as usual, raced on ahead, swishing a clear path into the forest with a hastily improvised cutlass.

'There has to be a reason for making everyone believe that it's all the work of the Howling Hag,' I said. 'Making up a legend, getting children involved so they can't breathe a word. It's clever. But why? Why do it at all? D'you know, I think if we could work that out we'd know who's behind it. You are really good at reading people, Raven. Think!'

Raven chewed the inside of her mouth and whispered that she didn't know. 'Mr Odorless was our best suspect,' she said so quietly I barely heard.

'I bet you do know, you just need to think it through. You worried it was Rookery, Morti was convinced it was Odorless. Maybe we need to go back over the curses again. I know some of it was to get everyone to believe there was a witch. Even that witch bottle tied to the front of the school, I now reckon that was the Howling Hag herself. But does anyone actually benefit from any of it? Who would want everyone at school obeying their orders? Henry's picture being destroyed, Sam hurting his hand? Who,' I finished, 'would want to kill Mr Pickles?'

'What was the word you used back in Tidy House?' Raven asked.

'Ah, that. Yes. I could tell that's what you were doing. You could have warned me. I don't know the proper word for it.'

Raven looked at me. She really didn't know what she'd been doing.

'Things talk to you, don't they? You can read an object's history. Thought transference. And you do it with people too. You look for the good and you can see it, even when it's quite hidden. But it's so natural to you, you don't even notice you're doing it. You see secrets too. I think the word is "scryer". Heard of that? It's your affinity, Raven. And you're a really good one.'

'Reading things. Seeing something good and

something secret,' she repeated. 'That's an affinity?' She stopped. 'That's my affinity?'

'Absolutely. I think your sadness at losing Snapdragon, then suffering Mr Odorless's raging, plus your worry about Rookery, really took the shine off your powers developing, just as they should've been showing themselves.'

'Well,' she carried on walking, 'it's true. I was afraid of just about everything.'

'Being a bit afraid is not so bad. People who don't take magic seriously are the ones likely to get their ears blown off.' I fell into step alongside her. 'But who knows what magic you might be able to do now that you've reached that magical part inside of you. Being a scryer makes you rare and pretty special. Plus it's a gift that kind of makes you a super-powered detective.'

We were close to the den now. Everyone wanted this to stop. And Raven was exactly the sort of person who could see behind all the smoke and mirrors the Howling Hag had set up.

'Come on. Who is the Howling Hag really? You need to confront the witch – or, not witch. We don't just need her to own up to what she's been doing. We need to get Snapdragon back and we need her to stop.'

Raven nodded. The mutter of low voices told me we'd reached the secret den. I slipped away on to a high branch to listen. And to think.

Sam beamed as Raven and Morti walked in. His eyes became wider with every sentence as Morti explained how Mr Odorless had walked in and caught Raven red-handed searching his home. Sam looked at Raven as if he had never been so impressed with anyone in his life.

'And you really just calmly walked out of there?'

'I think I probably would have screamed,' Ella admitted.

'So Mr Odorless is not the Howling Hag?' Henry voiced the disappointment they must all feel.

'Then who is?' said Bianca. 'Have we really no idea? I think she's just too clever and too powerful.'

Morti explained that being a detective was never that easy.

'Guess we wait until the fire ceremony,' said Henry practically. 'We lie in wait. We all know now the Howling Hag isn't really a witch. Someone just puts those notes inside hollow sticks. Someone must get there early to set it all up. We just need to be there even earlier and catch them right at it.'

'That means waiting nearly a whole week,' protested Ella.

'And school just keeps getting worse,' complained Morti. 'Everyone's jumpy and if Odorless doesn't get his way and we finally beat Fivetors at something I think he will explode just as surely as one of Miss Percy's experiments.'

'Actually,' said Raven in a small voice. I could tell she was being brave speaking out in front of a crowd like this. 'There's something that I think will make things better at school. Because it's not just the Howling Hag that makes school a bad place. Morti's right – Mr Odorless is obsessed with us never being as good as Fivetors at anything. And he just stomps around in a rage ruining things for everyone. But I think I know why.'

It was great to see Raven taking charge like this, and my ears pricked up as much as anyone's as she explained she now understood Mr Odorless and what made him so grumpy and cross.

'I've found out his secret.'

'A secret?' Sam was interested right away.

'What possible secret can he have that makes him behave like a big joy-sucking leech?' Ella wanted to know.

'And what can we do about it?' asked Carsen.

'Sam, remember all those newspaper cuttings in his office – they're all about how marvellous Fivetors is.'

'Yeah, but everyone knows he's obsessed with us beating them in something,' agreed Sam.

'There was something important about all those articles. They were all pictures of the super-successful head of Fivetors. He's got a seriously major crush,' explained Raven. 'He's in love with Miss Earnest.'

'That's just gross!' said Sam.

'Disgusting,' agreed Carsen.

'That is so sweeeet,' said Ella.

'Mr Odorless in love?' queried Bianca disbelievingly.

'It's not that he wants to beat Fivetors, it's that he wants to impress Miss Earnest. He desperately wants to be the best at something,' said Raven. 'I think anything would do. He's got pictures of Miss Earnest's achievements at home too. He constantly feels he will never be good enough to pluck up the courage to speak to her. What he needs is a boost to his confidence.'

She sounded as if she had a plan, but I couldn't see how the children could possibly help with this.

Carsen groaned. 'You're not going to say we all have to get better at our spelling and pass loads of tests, are you?'

Raven shook her head. 'We may not be able to stop the Howling Hag for few more days yet. But I do think we can stop Mr Odorless being so grumpy and spoiling our fun.' She looked around her. 'We'll need to work together. My plan is about a test. But it won't be anything to do with spelling.'

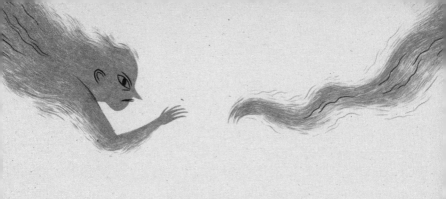

PART FIVE

37. NOT BEING SECOND BEST

Bianca was searching for the lid of the second biscuit tin she'd brought from home, but everyone else, the whole bunch who had turned up from school – Aaliyah, Carsen, Ella, Henry and Sam – headed off with Morti, going over the plan. I didn't need Raven's powers to tell it was the first time he'd had a gang of friends like this and he was really loving it.

The branches on the tree above the den were not as good as the ones in the hanging tree. But comfort-

able enough for doing one of the many things I do very well; I stayed on a high-up branch, watching and listening. Once everyone else had gone, a stillness descended, apart from Bianca rustling leaves behind tree-trunk seats, still searching for the missing half of her tin.

Raven had hung around. 'It was very kind of you to bring the biscuits. I think they've all been eaten. Sorry.'

Then Raven handed Bianca the lid from behind her back, as if the little witch had hidden it somewhere deliberately to keep Bianca behind.

'No trouble,' smiled Bianca. 'Everyone said they were the best biscuits.'

'What do you think will happen?' said Raven. 'When we turn up early at the fire ceremony and unmask the Howling Hag? That would be a really humiliating way for this to be over. Everyone wants this to stop.'

'Do they?' Bianca was pressing the lid down firmly and not looking at Raven. 'I think everyone knows the Howling Hag has been very clever. She's made us all do a few good dares. Mine was fun. It's made school much more exciting.'

There might be something in that. I'd heard them swapping notes about what the Howling Hag had challenged them to do – and they'd all been showing off, implying their curse was braver or more daring than any others. But no one was owning up to the horrible killing of Mr Pickles.

'Everyone would miss seeing what they can get away with.' Bianca turned to go. 'Life is more exciting with the Howling Hag.'

'No!' Raven said very firmly. Bianca stopped and turned. 'People don't like being told what to do. And they don't like being scared into it. You know it has to stop.'

'I don't think the Howling Hag is going to stop. Besides, no one can make her. She has powers. She *is* a witch, you know.'

'She really doesn't have powers,' said Raven quietly. 'But she does have my music box and I want it back.'

'How are you going to make her do that? You can't make the Howling Hag do anything she doesn't want to. She is so powerful. Besides, there is no evidence, not a thing, to show who she really is. So anything you say will just be a guess. You and Morti agreed. She is too clever. She is super-secret and super-clever and that's because she has superpowers.'

Raven took a step closer to Bianca. 'When people start to get away with things, they start to believe they have power – magical or not. They start to think they are invincible. And they make mistakes. Your mistake was going after my music box.'

'Mistakes! The Howling Hag has been amazing!' responded Bianca with a dazzling smile and a sweep of her luxuriant hair.

'There is no Howling Hag,' Raven went on quietly. 'It's all you! And you have no powers.'

Bianca Maudlin? I'd known Raven could work it out. I kept very still in the tree, wanting to hear every word. Was Bianca really the Howling Hag?

'You have given yourself away. Because you don't look much at other people, do you? You think of yourself and how people see you. But each time anyone has drawn their curse out of the fire, they've burnt their fingers.' Raven grabbed Bianca's hands.

Bianca tried to snatch away her hands, but Raven held on. 'I haven't once seen you with plasters, Bianca. Yet you said you'd enjoyed doing your curse. Your mum is even in charge of plasters – you could have put on a couple to pretend so easily that you got your curse out of the fire. That makes it doubly stupid. That means it's over.'

'That's not evidence. It's nonsense!' Bianca snatched away her hands. 'There is no proof who the Howling Hag is. She is way too clever for you.'

I had a bad feeling Bianca was right. We really hadn't a shred of evidence. I could listen intently – but I'd never be able to speak up and share anything I heard. And she wasn't going to admit it anyway.

My whiskers trembled. I willed Raven to press on – hoping Bianca would relish the chance to show off how clever she had been and give herself away in the process.

We needed proof. I began to think that might be up to me.

'Here's the deal,' went on Raven. 'Just give me the music box back and I'll keep your secret. No one need know it was you who did that awful thing to lovely Mr Pickles.'

Bianca dipped under the low branch, ready to leave and still smiling. But Raven just kept on talking.

'It was mostly about making you feel powerful, making everyone scared there was a witch cursing and controlling the school. But there is more evidence. I worked it out that someone benefited directly from some of the curses. You didn't like everyone admiring Ella's shoes – you think everything you have is the best. Henry's picture got ruined, but it had beaten yours into second place. What did you do – cut the string only a bit so if you

305

got lucky it would crash when no one was near and everyone would whisper and say it was magic?'

'Sounds clever to me, not lucky,' said Bianca. 'The Hag planned it perfectly. Just proves she has powers. Anyway, I don't even bother with Photography Club any more, not since I realized they're not very good judges. The Howling Hag is so powerful, she even got strutting Sam to go along with finally not winning *everything*. And I won the tennis trophy because I am very good at tennis.'

'Bianca, honestly, you have a strange idea of what makes you popular.'

'Sam's really popular and he wins at everything,' pointed out Bianca.

'But he wins fairly. And he's great to have on a team. You might have won the tennis trophy this time, but you only did it by making sure Sam didn't win. You won't be popular if I have to tell everyone about your tricks and cheating. So I am giving you a choice. It doesn't have to end with everyone knowing. The Howling Hag could just fade away.'

There was a short silence. Raven carried on.

'When Ella was so upset about her special stone going missing, you found her a better one. You can be kind. I'm asking you to be kind now. Either you go straight away and bring me my music box, or I explain what's been happening, starting with your parents.'

'And what would you say?'

'I would tell everyone that as well as stealing my music box, you did one of the most terrible curses. Why did Mr Pickles have to die?'

'Not me. The Howling Hag.' Bianca hesitated a fraction. She licked her lips. 'Seeing as it's only us here, I may as well tell you.' Her face curled into a smile. 'I'm glad about what happened to Mr Pickles. Everyone loved stupid Mr Pickles, thought he was *so cute*. But I really hated him. He was always having a go at me for not sharing. So Mum insisted on buying him those awful bloomers to say sorry for *him* being rude to *me*. In front of the whole class.'

Raven took a step closer. 'Please do this the easy way, Bianca, or I'll have to tell everyone. Everyone will know the truth about the Howling Hag – that it was never about larks and dares. It was just about you. You cheated to win at tennis. And you ruined a picture that was better than yours, and humiliated Ella. You have been clever, but the music box was a mistake. Because you wanted to keep that for yourself. Makes you a thief.'

'You have absolutely zero proof. It's your word against mine.' Bianca was still brazening it out.

'Rookery gave me that music box. She wanted me to have it because it's very old and you really can't buy anything like it and I'm very special and everyone wants me to be to be their best friend. I have the best parties, everyone knows that. She is very lucky.'

'I think you should try harder to appreciate what a wonderful person Rookery is.'

Bianca leant forwards, looking desperate and eager. 'My mum believes your grandmother was a real witch. The only way for measly Ella to have got that goal was magic. Rookery has this look sometimes.' Bianca took a step closer to Raven. 'Does she really have powers?'

I couldn't say for sure if Rookery would have confessed her secret to her new best friend. But Finch had drummed it into those girls to always Deny Everything.

'Of course she doesn't have powers,' Raven replied slickly, as if she'd been Denying Everything every day of her life. 'She's just kind, like her grandma. Anyone can do extraordinary things if people believe in them. You are incredibly lucky to have her as a best friend. This is your last chance not to ruin it, to ruin everything, Bianca. All I want is my music box back.'

'Rookery does too have powers, but she doesn't

use them for anything in the slightest bit useful. I have powers too! I am so powerful I can stamp my foot and I can open up a huge crack in the world and make you disappear into it.'

I saw Raven glance uneasily at the ground. All around the earth was cracked and it didn't take much to imagine one of those fissures opening into a vast dark hole. The fact that Bianca was not backing down was making Raven unsure. And if there is one thing all magical people know, it's almost impossible to tell just by looking at someone if they have magic. It wasn't difficult to believe Bianca really did have powers. She had manipulated the entire school into believing in the Howling Hag's curses. She was brimming with confidence.

Bianca took a threatening stance. 'Don't mess with me.'

As she stepped forward, Raven retaliated with pure instinct, like the true witch she was. She swept her arms across herself and without even touching Bianca, the girl went flying back into the trunk of the tree. I saw Raven look at her hands, not able to believe what she had just done, channelling some of her psychic energy like that. I could see small curls of smoke issuing from the tips of her fingers, but they were gone in an instant.

Bianca was a little dusty and more than a little shocked.

'Now, my music box,' said Raven, standing over her, but also offering a hand to help her to her feet. 'Fetch it, get back here and hand it over. I am giving you ten minutes.'

Bianca dusted herself down and left without another word.

But I simply did not trust her enough to be sure what was going to happen next.

38. TO BE A STEALTH CAT

I hadn't exaggerated – well, not much – about the fact that I'd cleared up some tricky cases of sorcerers-gone-bad. Bad humans are not so very different. I knew what was likely to happen and my senses were alert that this was not yet over.

Bianca had been used to people at school looking up to her. Dreaming up the legend of the Howling Hag had not only been clever, but it must have made her feel invincible.

Raven was a nice human. She couldn't see what I

could – that Bianca had a taste of real power and wasn't going to let it go. There was fight in her and that music box was our only real evidence.

I had one idea that might work.

Just as I was about to climb down from my perch, determined to keep Bianca Maudlin in my sight, a small movement, deep in the shadowy recesses of the den, stopped me.

Whiskers and white mice! Rookery Charming. But Rookery had left with everyone else. Hadn't she? That girl had such a stillness about her, an ability to almost become part of the shadows, that I'd almost say she could become invisible. She had been standing completely still. She must have heard every word.

Without a moment's hesitation, Raven rushed over and gave her sister the world's biggest hug, as if they hadn't seen each other in a long time.

'You are the best, Rookery,' Raven said. 'I know all you really want is to be normal, just like my whole life all I've wanted is to have powers like you. We're opposites, aren't we? I always want your straight dark hair instead of my brown curly hair and I want your patience. No one else would be nice enough to untangle Everly's kite from the tree. Bianca fooled everyone.'

Rookery didn't lift her head from Raven's

shoulder. 'But I'm not nice. I mostly wanted to be friends with Bianca because I get to help with all her pets. That makes me just as bad, wanting something from her.'

'Never, Rookery, you could never be a bad person.'

'Then how come I'm the one with the magic, all the power, but you're the one who stood up to her? I took your music box without telling you and I knew that was wrong. Bianca was right about my powers – what's the point of having them if you don't use them? You've sorted out everything, you've stopped the Howling Hag – and you haven't even used magic.'

I would have clapped. But it's one thing you really cannot do with paws. My place was to keep a tight watch on Bianca. I darted along in her footsteps. We hadn't stopped the Howling Hag, not yet. I was going to need to be a stealth cat.

Luckily, I am always a stealth cat.

39. Pistols at the Ready

Raven waited with Rookery, looking anxiously along the path for any signs of Bianca returning with the music box. The ten minutes were up and Raven strode along the path towards the high street, Rookery trailing.

'Don't worry, Raven,' Rookery was trying to reassure her. 'I'm sure Bianca won't want everyone to know she was the Howling Hag. She'll bring it.'

But there was no sign of Bianca. Outside the village inn a bunch of the children had gathered.

Morti was holding his water gun and Raven heard him suggest everyone head home, get their best soakers and to head to Beechy Wood for a massive water fight.

'We can meet by the dragon tree – you know the one? Lots of trees look like they're going to come alive and maybe eat you, but that's just trees, that's just part of the fun of woods. There is basically no reason to be scared of Beechy Wood. The dragon tree is my favourite tree, does anyone else have a favourite?'

Raven found herself giving a little smile. Only a few days ago, Morti had been scared of the creaking noise made by a few branches rubbing together.

And then she saw Bianca! Relief! She was striding towards them from her house at the top of Twinhills. She had taken the trouble to put on her super-smart best sparkly hairband and her glossy straight hair swung perfectly behind her. She walked as if she owned the whole of Twinhills. The high street was suddenly deserted as everyone dispersed to their houses to collect things for the water fight.

Bianca wasn't carrying anything.

'Where's my music box?' demanded Raven, not even trying to keep the anger out of her voice.

'You two can't bully me into having everything your own way,' said Bianca as she reached the sisters.

'In the end it's my word against yours, because you have no proof.'

Raven's stomach was completely queasy.

'You can't prove I have your stupid music box,' Bianca said. And she turned, her hair flying like a glossy flag behind her. Like this was over.

Raven watched her starting to walk away and could not think of a single thing she could do to stop her. Bianca was right. It was Raven's word against hers and so far Bianca had been more clever and more devious than Raven had even imagined.

Raven wanted to yell out to anyone who would listen that Bianca was the Howling Hag. But the high street was deserted and all Bianca's defiant words and denials came back to her. What proof did they have? And would that get the music box back? That was the most important thing. So far, Bianca had outsmarted them.

The thought of confessing everything to Mum was terrible. As Bianca walked away, she glanced back, unable to stop a smile of triumph writing itself on her face. There was nothing Raven could do or say to make her stop.

But there was a small, dark shape coming towards them. A black shape, low to the ground, like a puddle of liquid darkness. Nightshade was slow and struggling, because held firmly in her jaws was the sparkly red handbag that matched the hairband Bianca was wearing.

Bianca's face flickered as she saw the cat approaching.

'What are you doing with that, Snoozy?' Bianca demanded, her face immediately losing its defiant look. 'Have you . . . have you been in my room?' She swung round to face Raven again. 'Has that cat been spying on me all this time? And we've been nice to it, and fed it.'

Nightshade looked relieved to drop the handbag at Raven's feet.

Raven crouched down to open the bag, fingers trembling. She guessed that the smart cat had known Bianca would try to double-cross them. And she hoped that Nightshade had finally found them some evidence.

But Bianca was not going to stand there and let Raven discover exactly what Nightshade had found hidden in her room. Bianca moved quickly, and before Raven could get the bag open, shoved her out of the way. But as Bianca tried to pick up the bag, she struggled as if an invisible force was keeping her away from it. Raven could see her sister's eyes had turned a little grey and smoky.

Raven opened the bag and lifted out the music box, her hands shaking, afraid of dropping it, aware that all her friends were returning, one by one, with water pistols at the ready.

As much as she wanted to, she daren't open the box now to make sure Snapdragon was safe. She just brought it to her chest and clung on to it.

Rookery released her magical hold on Bianca, who moved forward to try to seize the music box, but Raven dodged away.

'Rookery gave me that music box,' said Bianca to everyone assembled in a circle around them. 'Raven's being very mean and jealous. You can't take it back. It was a gift. That is stealing, Raven Charming.'

Raven was wrong-footed again. She hadn't foreseen just how determined Bianca really was.

Nightshade was miaowing loudly. Raven was getting the big eyes, and thought she understood. There was something else in the sparkly bag. She reached inside once again and pulled out a small blue cap with the words 'I ♥ Cheese' embroidered on it.

'What are you doing with Mr Pickles' hat?' asked Henry.

'Where did you get that, that was in my . . .' stuttered Bianca.

'That means you killed Mr Pickles!' said Aaliyah.

'You're the Howling Hag!' accused Carsen.

'That bag isn't mine, I've never seen it before in my life.'

'Actually, I've seen you with it a few times,' said Ella.

'And it exactly matches the hairband you're wearing,' pointed out Henry. 'I think this is justice for Mr Pickles.'

'And you've got your music box back, good,' Ella said to Raven.

'Does that mean the end of the Howling Hag?' Aaliyah looked anxiously but hopefully at Raven.

'Yep. It's all over,' answered Sam. 'We all know now, don't we?' He had the biggest water gun and shouldered it. 'Sure, you had fun being the Howling Hag while it lasted, but we don't want to do that any more. You try any more tricks, Bianca, and it'll be game over for you. We'll be watching you.'

'Poor Mr Pickles,' sighed Ella. 'Don't you think we should report her? Let everyone know she's the one behind all the scare stories? That she murdered Mr Pickles.'

Bianca just stood there, not finding anything to say.

'Please don't,' said Aaliyah. 'I can put back the

stone and Sian's twenty pounds now. I don't want to have to admit she made me steal. As Sam says, it's over. That's what's important.'

Sam fixed Bianca with a stern look. 'OK, Bianca? Understood? You can join in with us, if you want to. But you're going to need to bring your own water gun.'

They all turned and began to walk towards Beechy Wood. It really was over. Raven finally relaxed, a little bit too soon. Bianca made one, final desperate lunge for the music box, seizing it before Raven could react.

Then, just as quickly, Rookery's magic box lifted cleanly out of Bianca's hands. And without even thinking, Raven crossed her arms and black smoke swirled around Bianca's ankles. She landed with a thump on her backside on the grass by the side of the road.

'Your magic is a lot angrier than mine,' whispered Rookery to Raven under her breath, as Rookery took back the precious box.

Raven's eyes cleared and the smoke blew away almost instantly.

But Morti and the others had watched the whole thing.

There was silence. Was everyone wondering just

how Bianca had ended up on the floor? Without anyone touching her?

Morti spoke quickly: 'Amazing, the moves Rookery learns from ballet. And their grandpa teaches 'em yoga. That one was so quick I hardly saw it. Wow. OK – Beechy Wood, now. You all better be ready for this.'

'I was born ready,' answered Henry, racing after Morti with a gun even bigger and a more startling shade of pink than Ella's.

Rookery, Raven and Bianca watched them all leave.

'It really is over, Bianca,' Raven said. 'You may as well go join in with the water fight. You're lucky anyone wants to be friends with you after everything you've done. But if you still want to help, you know the plan for tomorrow, and everyone is relying on you to play your part.'

With a trembling lip, Bianca nodded.

40. A TRAY OF JAM TARTS

Mum leapt up from her desk the moment they arrived at Sundial Cottage – she clearly had not been concentrating on her work. Knox emerged from the kitchen with a fresh tray of jam tarts.

'I hope everyone is hungry. I've been baking to take my mind off waiting. This is the third batch.' His hair was looking quite dishevelled. He gave an anxious glance at Mum, who must have contacted Knox and alerted him that there might be some news on Snapdragon.

Rookery was carrying the music box and approached Mum's desk. Raven's stomach felt uncomfortably fluttery, hoping Snapdragon was going to be all right, that she hadn't come to any harm being constantly woken by her granddaughter and then being kidnapped by a fake witch.

Mum swept away two spell books, some newish-looking scrolls, and a slab of very tasty-looking chocolate sat next to a little black bottle of poison. It did tend to put you off breaking off even a little piece of the chocolate.

Then there was a thundering knock on the door that made everyone look around. Raven went to answer.

Morti was in the doorway, breathing hard as if he had been running. He said in a whisper loud enough so everyone heard. 'I know about Deny Everything and I know that your mum mustn't know I know. But I *really* want to know what's happening.'

He was dripping wet and clutching his giant orange water soaker, which was drizzling water too. Raven knew Morti had dragged himself away from a great game to come and find her. She shooed him inside and watched Rookery slide the music box into the space Mum created on her desk. Mum was looking curiously at Morti and frowned as Nightshade slid in behind him.

'It's fine, Mum,' said Raven as Rookery went to fuss over Nightshade. 'Morti is a friend and I trust him. It makes you fearful and messes everything up if you feel you can't trust anyone enough to tell the truth. So he pretty much knows everything.'

Mum opened her mouth, so Raven pressed on. 'You keep telling me being talented at magic is not the most important thing and now I know it's true. And what about Dad? When did you tell him you were a sorcerer? When did that come up, exactly?'

Mum shut her mouth with a snap.

'Did someone mention me?'

The next figure to come through the front door was big enough to envelop both his children in a familiar hug, familiar even with a scratchy beard and a strange smell of air fresheners and plastic-wrapped sandwiches that spoke to Raven of a long journey.

'Dad!' they chorused.

'Wow, you smell better than I do. You smell of the forest, you two. You haven't smelt like this for months. I thought you were getting too grown up to go climbing trees. Probably means I've got you both the wrong presents.'

'Presents!' Just for a moment Raven forgot all about Snapdragon.

Dad looked around at a crowded Sundial Cottage. 'I'd have brought more presents if I'd known there was going to be a welcoming party.'

'Have a jam tart,' said Knox.

Dad took two, saying he hadn't eaten home-cooked food in ages. He was introduced to Morti, who said hello through a mouthful of jam tart, and Nightshade. Then he went to hug Mum, who had been hopping from one leg to the other.

'Presents?' repeated Rookery, looking hopefully at the wheeled suitcase Dad had dragged in behind him, on which sat some impressively large boxes.

'Raven was in the middle of telling us something important, but it's wonderful to have you home,' said Mum as Dad's gaze fell on the desk, cleared except for the music box.

'Well, I guess it's presents later,' he said, turning to Raven. 'Carry on.' He went and sat heavily on one of Snapdragon's awful tapestry cushions. Raven thought she heard a tiny miaow from somewhere.

She reminded herself where she had got to and glanced at Mum, who said: 'OK, Morti's a friend. He can stay. But that cat is riddled with magic. It might be dangerous.'

Raven's eyes met Nightshade's big green ones. She hesitated over telling Mum that Nightshade could speak. After all, that was Nightshade's secret.

'Mum, you can only investigate Nightshade's magic if she says she wants you to,' insisted Raven.

'And how am I going to know if she gives me permission?' said Mum, placing her hands on her desk.

'Don't worry, I'll tell you,' responded Nightshade quickly.

'Exactly, glad that's cleared up,' said Raven.

'I'd say that doesn't even begin to clear things up,' grinned Dad from the sofa. 'I can tell I'm behind on quite a lot of things.'

Mum raised an eyebrow at Nightshade, who delicately lapped a bowl of milk and nibbled a jam tart Rookery had fetched for her.

'Raven was being very sensible.' Mum glanced at Dad. 'Saying, what's the point of having a talent like being magical if it just shuts you off and makes you fearful of things everyone else enjoys as being normal, like having friends.'

'Quite right. I think normal is over-rated,' said Nightshade. 'You can leave normal to everyone else. It's a very good idea to have a few friends who are different from you. Like cats. Helps you get an alternative perspective on life.'

'Now, please, let me know about Snapdragon,'

said Mum as Knox handed around more jam tarts.

'This is about your grandma?' said Dad. 'We all thought . . .' He scratched at his stubbly chin. He badly needed a shave. 'We . . . What did we think?'

Raven lifted the music box. She stopped focusing on how close she had come to losing Snapdragon again, and repeated the story her grandma had told her. How she had been encased in a bubble charm, floating to the top of the hanging tree to fetch ingredients for charms she was carrying in a satchel, including one for Mrs Maudlin, who was sad Little Miss Tweets had never recovered her voice after a severe case of bird flu. Raven gently felt underneath the box for the winder, turning it four times, and placed it back in the centre of Mum's desk as she was reaching the end of the story.

Raven kept her fingers crossed as the first notes of 'Danse Macabre' started up and the black triangles on the top of the box began to twitch.

She continued, about how Snapdragon had spied one of the Maudlins' naughty runaway kittens and then disaster had struck. She'd lost control of the bubble charm and had the presence of mind to do a swift hiding spell to take her to safety. But she must have been hit first by goodness knows what mix of spells, which reacted as she tumbled out of the tree.

Everyone moved in close, forming a circle of noses around the music box. But Raven was the most nervous of anyone. Would her grandma still be OK?

As the black triangles slid back to reveal a dark opening, up rose the miniature Snapdragon, snoring little delicate snores. And Knox burst into tears.

41. DANSE MACABRE

'But how on earth did you find her?' asked Dad, munching one of the last of the cookies Rookery had made for his return.

'She's a scryer,' said Nightshade.

Dad gave a shifty look at Nightshade, as if he didn't quite trust getting this information by talking to a cat. But Raven had discovered that talking wasn't even the most remarkable thing about Nightshade.

'I can touch objects and people and I can tell things about them,' said Raven simply. 'And I can

even channel some of that psychic energy, but that definitely needs a lot of work.' Raven licked jam from her fingers. 'My affinity.'

'You've discovered your affinity and channelled psychic energy? I haven't been gone all that long!' said Dad. 'But I feel I've been away ages. There is only one thing I can say. Presents!'

Mum had looked out for something small enough to put in a restorative spell for Snapdragon. A dark-green potion waited next to the music box in a thimble. They'd need Snapdragon wide awake to help them break the spells she'd been hit with. If she could remember.

Raven unwrapped her gift and could not believe what Dad had brought her. A beautiful music box, inlaid with many different types of wood, just like the one in which Snapdragon had hidden. She was speechless.

'It's not a beautiful antique like Snapdragon's,' apologized Dad. 'But I always knew you loved hers and I've been planning on getting you one of your own for ages. And I managed to take a day off from the conference because I'd heard there was a music box maker and it was this incredible journey . . . Anyway, I can tell you the whole story later. But it even plays the same tune.'

'It's beautiful,' breathed Raven, lifting the lid and hearing the high, tinny version of 'Danse Macabre'.

'And Rookery, I decided there was something missing from your life that I think every witch needs.' He placed a cardboard box on the floor in front of her.

Rookery opened it and took out an impossibly small, impossibly fluffy black kitten who miaowed with a tiny pink mouth. Nightshade gave a disdainful look.

'I am not giving Rookery a cat because I think she's more of a witch than you,' Dad said to Raven. 'I just think she's more keen to have a pet.'

'I know that,' answered Raven. 'And you are right.'

'You're just the best for knowing exactly what everyone needs,' said Mum. 'Raven takes so much after you. But Raven!' Mum was peering at the tiny sleeping form of Snapdragon, as if she really wanted to prod her awake and let her know she was the centre of a lot of excited attention. 'Your affinity? How did you discover that?'

'I guess I've always been able to read people. I just thought it was how everyone was. It was Nightshade who told me I did it well enough for it to be magic.'

'She reads objects as well,' said Rookery. 'Not just people.'

Rookery fussed over the kitten and found it a bit of string to play with. Nightshade stalked off to sit in a sunny patch by the window, pink nose in the air as if such games were far too frivolous.

'Well, it's a very useful skill,' said Knox, wiping his eyes, 'because I guess that's how you found Snapdragon.'

'I guess it is,' said Raven.

'So – with you being an expert and all, can you fix Snapdragon?' asked Morti, asking the question that everyone else had only been thinking.

'Fix?' asked Nightshade, green eyes gleaming from the window.

Mum started chewing the end of her glasses and saying that Snapdragon might remember what was in the spells that broke around her.

'Guess that bracelet of yours will help,' said Morti, standing very close to the pile of jam tarts. Raven offered him another. 'But we've got good clues for some of it, haven't we?' he said through his contented chewing. 'And my detecting skills tell me it solves another mystery.'

'*Another* mystery?' sighed Dad. 'What mystery does it solve?'

Morti's face screwed up. 'Snapdragon was making a spell to bring Little Miss Tweets' voice back. So that's one charm we know was in her satchel. And we know that she stopped halfway up to speak to a kitten that had escaped from the Maudlins'. Mrs M knocked on every door in Twinhills looking for homes for all them naughty kittens. So it might not just have been Snapdragon who got hit by a rogue spell.' He looked pointedly at Nightshade.

'You think . . . ?' Raven turned to where Nightshade was sunning herself. 'Nightshade, what did you say brought you to Twinhills?'

'Seth thought I should have a holiday and thought I'd be at home here as . . . Oh, yes, his father got me from someone in Twinhills who was looking for homes for a load of kittens. This is where I was born.'

'You think Nightshade was the kitten Snapdragon saw?' said Rookery, dragging a piece of wool and watching her own kitten follow it in tiny leaps. 'She got hit by the voice spell when Snapdragon fell?'

Raven looked at Nightshade, her eyes shining. 'Nightshade, you really have taught Morti to be an amazing detective. He's right – that's how you can talk.'

Nightshade got nervously to her feet and shook out her paws. 'It all sounds very plausible. I'd say he's an honorary detecto-cat,' she agreed gruffly, making

Morti blush to the tips of his ears. She turned to Finch, who was already twirling her bracelet. 'But you are not coming anywhere near me with that.'

'I could fix you,' Finch said. 'It was all Snapdragon's mistake. I could unpick the accidental magic you were cursed with.'

'Cursed? There is nothing about me that needs fixing, thank you very much,' said Nightshade. And she was gone, out of an open window.

'Well. Operation Pickles is all solved,' said Morti in a voice tinged with sadness. 'It was a lot more complicated than any of us were expecting. And we set out to find the Howling Hag and ended up finding Snapdragon. I guess you were right from the start, Raven. There is only one magical family in Twinhills. Now, an epic battle awaits.' He headed for the door, but paused. 'I don't suppose I could recharge my ammo . . . from your tap? And just thinking . . . you've got quite a stash of jam tarts here. We'd gladly help out . . .'

Knox went to fetch a tin, just as Morti added, 'Look – your grandma's waking up. You'd better see if whatever spell you've got in that thimble wakes her up properly. I guess fixing that horrible mix of spells she hit herself with as will be the biggest curse-breaking challenge of your life, Mrs Charming.'

42. OPERATION SUNFLOWER

This was supposed to have been a holiday, but my snoozetime was seriously depleted and what I actually needed was another holiday to get over it. But Morti was wrong about one thing. There was still one more important mission before Operation Pickles was finally over.

'Not Operation Pickles, this one should have an operation name all of its own,' said Morti, as we headed up to the school on Sunday morning.

Raven was unusually silent, even her walk not

quite as bouncy as expected, seeing as most of her troubles were over. There was quite a gathering outside the school.

I'd expected Ella, Aaliyah, Sam, Carsen and Henry. Rookery too. But I was pleased that Bianca Maudlin had chosen to show her face. She was keeping her chin up and had brought another batch of biscuits, which were proving popular. I'd predicted she'd have persuaded her parents to put their house up for sale and move out of Twinhills quicker than you could say Mr Pickles. Looks like I was wrong.

Everyone was kind, they always were, giving me pats on the head or a tickle under the chin. But it was a constant difficulty to remember not to talk, particularly when I was very overdue a well-earned nap. I badly needed that holiday.

News had spread, as news did very quickly in Twinhills, that the children had cooked up a plan between them to try to make the school a bit more fun. And how it all hinged on making sure Twinhills finally won at something.

Most of the children had shown up and flooded in once the gates were opened. They'd been lured here by the promise of seeing some miracle that would turn Mr Odorless into a much less angry person. If there was one thing I was sure of, it was that Raven Charming understood people very well. If anyone could find a way to transform the head teacher, she could.

Mr Odorless looked pretty perplexed by such overwhelming and enthusiastic support. Never had there been such a turnout for the judging of the Fivetors and Twinhills Tallest Sunflower Prize. He had started turning a worried purple already.

'Is this really going to make a difference?' Sam asked Raven again. He had been sceptical about the whole plan, but she stayed firm, said she had everything organized and under control, and ordered him to race on ahead as we all took up our positions.

I watched her take a deep breath.

The judge was the Supreme Head of the Fivetors and Twinhills Annual Horticultural Carnival (Mrs Chin, Aaliyah's mum, who ran the village shop). She was accompanied by the impressive head of Fivetors, Miss Earnest, tall as a sunflower herself. She swept through the school gates like a battleship with guns ready to fire on both sides. Mrs Chin scuttled behind wearing a colourful scarf that was blowing in the stiff breeze. It was threatening to take off like Everly's kite and end up tangled in the top of the hanging tree.

Mr Odorless was wearing a freshly brushed suit

and had got himself a haircut. He looked nervous as he approached Mrs Chin, who was gripping on to her clipboard and her tape measure tightly, as if they might be blown away.

This was where Bianca had to play her part, and I heard Raven take another steadying breath, hoping she had judged this entire operation correctly.

I knew she didn't really trust Bianca, but unless she could get the girl to feel part of Twinhills, rather than seeing everything as a competition where she deserved to come out on top, she was always going to be at war.

Raven had struggled her whole life trying not to let people down, worrying so much about others and feeling she didn't belong. Perhaps Raven could teach Bianca a little about how to think about other people.

As Mrs Chin and Miss Earnest were ready for the walk to the pond, Bianca stepped forwards, perfectly timed and exactly according to plan. Mr Odorless had been making some effusive welcome speech but Bianca interrupted him by offering round a plate of biscuits. She explained, in rather more detail than she needed to, how she had not bought them, but had made them herself specially.

Odorless's colour deepened at being interrupted,

but paled to the colour of a shrimp as Miss Earnest eagerly accepted a biscuit.

The operation relied on Bianca slowing them for long enough for Morti to get the crucial intel we needed – to see exactly what was written on that clipboard held by the Supreme Judge, who had been to judge the Fivetors sunflowers first.

We needed to know how we measured up. Was it cheating? Possibly. Sneaky? Definitely. But this was a battle for the future happiness of the school. Twinhills' pride, their chances of finally beating the bigger school at something, anything, depended on the crucial detail of the height of Fivetors' tallest sunflower – and making sure ours was taller.

There had been a few questions about this part of the plan. But Raven had been magnificent, just telling everyone to trust her. And never revealing that there was going to be magic involved. If anyone asked, she would Deny Everything beautifully, I knew.

The two women nibbled a biscuit each and listened to Bianca tell them the recipe. It gave Morti time. His head bobbed up over the wall behind them just long enough so he could read what was on the sheet with some spy glasses, get the insider information, then his head vanished again just as quickly.

Morti informed Sam, the fastest runner, Sam immediately raced down to the pond where Henry was waiting with a tape measure so we'd know the precise height of Twinhills' own sunflowers.

Raven's whole plan was to make Mr Odorless stop feeling second best at everything and being miserable about it. And to do that, Twinhills had to win at something – Mr Odorless's precious sunflowers were the first chance to do that.

Henry went about his measuring quickly while the judge and the heads of the two competing schools trod the path down to the pond.

But Henry was giving a sorry shake of his head. I watched him gesture, showing two with his hands and then putting his thumb down. Twinhills' tallest flower was two centimetres too short. They were going to lose to Fivetors. Again! The big heads of the sunflowers seemed to droop in shame.

Rookery was lurking, as she did so well, keeping almost invisibly to one side in the shade of the trees. I would bet no one would notice she was standing anywhere near. But she was near enough for what she secretly needed to do as the party reached the sunflowers.

I watched her eyes go just a little smoky at the moment Mrs Chin took out her tape measure. And the heads of the nodding sunflowers seemed to perk up just the tiniest bit, all standing just a little taller and prouder. Would Rookery's magic have done enough? Would anyone wonder how those sunflowers seemed to lift their heads at exactly the right moment? We just had to hope everyone would be so pleased with the outcome no one stopped to ask questions.

Mrs Chin wrote her numbers down on her clipboard, but kept the results to herself until the whole crowd of children, parents and others from the village had caught the atmosphere and had flooded through the school gates. All gathered in great anticipation. She cleared her throat.

'I'm pleased to announce that the winner of the Fivetors and Twinhills Tallest Sunflower Prize, by just two centimetres, is . . . Twinhills School!'

The biggest cheer went up. The entire school erupted. And nobody could have looked more surprised than Mr Odorless at the enormous celebration.

A *tiny* bit of cheating maybe. But for a very good cause.

Then Aaliyah came forward with flowers for Miss Earnest, and pointed at Mr Odorless saying they were a present from him, because her sunflowers had been very marvellous, even if they hadn't been quite as tall as Twinhills'.

It was called being magnanimous, Raven had explained to Bianca, who had sneered at the entire plan. At least Raven had resisted asking Bianca to spell it and put it into a sentence. And Bianca had helped to pick some really nice flowers.

Morti hadn't been convinced at all that the plan was going to work. 'Old Odorless is going to win the tallest sunflower competition. He's going to feel all worthy and we're going to pretend he's given her some poxy flowers. And that's it – they fall in love?'

'It's worth a go,' I said. 'Lots of things about you humans sound mad, but honestly, I watch you all the time and I think it will work. He just needs a confidence boost so he doesn't feel he's second best and not worthy to speak to Miss Earnest.'

I could predict from the shy way that Miss Earnest blushed as she accepted the flowers, and how Mr Odorless and she disappeared off for a little walk under the trees, that things might change for the better at Twinhills School.

Mr Odorless's face had changed again. But not to purple. He was smiling.

I predicted they'd be married within the month.

I might even come back and see it. Not as a guest of honour. Us cats, we have a part to play, but we don't expect thanks. Although a nice piece of fish would do, if you happen to have one lying around.

ACKNOWLEDGEMENTS

One of the great things about writing is the chance to work with so many talented and creative people, and all you learn from them.

Thank you very much to everyone at my publisher, Chicken House, for being so supportive of me and my writing. I have been so excited to bring this new story into the world and I know I am incredibly lucky to have such a brilliant team to work with, who have brought passion and imagination at every stage. It is great working with you.

The vital team extends to all the booksellers, librarians, teachers, authors and enthusiastic book lovers in so many countries. And the translators who manage to work out brilliant alternatives for all the things I twist and make up.

It is difficult to single out individuals; there are so many who work so hard and so tirelessly to help inspire the young readers of today. Where would we be without you all?

Thank you to the talented Héloïse Mab for the spooky yet beautiful cover design.

Thank you to my wonderful agent, Jo Hayes, for all her endless patience and wisdom.

The home team is just as important. Particular

thanks goes to my tech-team of Alex and Tim Thornton for all their brilliant help with all my virtual projects. I have such fun and have learnt so much from my exceedingly talented family. I appreciate you also being there with tea, hugs and celebrations as needed.

Huge thanks as always to Mark. You are where the team begins and what everything else is based on. Thank you for being the vital calm centre of a lot of chaos.